Thoughts

Giacomo Leopardi

Translated by J.G. Nichols

T0286513

ALMA CLASSICS

ALMA CLASSICS
an imprint of

ALMA BOOKS LTD
3 Castle Yard
Richmond
Surrey TW10 6TF
United Kingdom
www.almaclassics.com

Thoughts first published in Italian in 1837
This translation first published by Hesperus Press Ltd in 2002
First published in this revised version by Alma Books Ltd in 2017

Translation, Notes and Extra Material © J.G. Nichols 2002, 2017

Printed in Great Britain by CPI Group (UK) Ltd, Croydon CR0 4YY

ISBN: 978-1-84749-737-6

Contents

THOUGHTS

1

For a long time I have denied the truth of the things I am about to say, because, apart from the fact that they are utterly foreign to my nature (and we always tend to judge others by ourselves), I have never been inclined to hate people, but to love them. In the end experience has persuaded me, indeed almost forced me, to believe the truth of these things. And I am certain that those readers who happen to have had many and various dealings with human beings will admit the truth of what I am about to say. Everyone else will maintain that it is exaggerated, until experience, if they ever do have occasion to experience human society fully, brings them face to face with it.

I maintain that the world is a league of scoundrels against honest men, and of the contemptible against the high-minded. When two or more scoundrels find themselves together for the first time, they have no trouble in recognizing each other for what they are, almost as if they had signs upon them to point it out, and they are immediately at one, or, if their personal interests will not permit this, they certainly feel inclined towards each other, and have great respect for each other. If a scoundrel has dealings or business with other scoundrels, it often happens that he acts honestly and without deceit. If he is dealing with honourable people, it is impossible for him to be trustworthy, and whenever it is to his advantage, he will not hesitate to ruin them. He will do this even if they are spirited people, capable of taking their revenge, because he hopes that his tricks will get the better of their cleverness, as almost always is the case. More than once I have seen very frightened people, finding themselves caught between a scoundrel more frightened than they are and someone who is honest and full of courage, take the scoundrel's part out of fear. Indeed, this always happens when your average person finds himself in similar situations, because the ways of the brave and honest person are straightforward and well known, while those of the rogue are concealed and endlessly varied. Now, as everyone is aware, the unknown is much more frightening than what is known, and you can easily guard against the vengeance of the right-minded, because your own baseness and fear will save you from it. But no fear and no baseness can save you from secret persecution, from deceit, or even from the open attacks made on you by enemies who are themselves contemptible. In daily life true courage is generally little feared, simply because, since there is no imposture about it, it is without that ostentation which makes things frightening. Courage is often not believed in, while scoundrels are feared as though they were brave, because, by virtue of their impostures, they are frequently held to be brave.

Scoundrels are seldom poor. Apart from anything else, if an honest man falls into poverty, no one gives him any aid, and many rejoice at it, while on the other hand, if a rogue becomes poor, everyone gathers round to help him. The reason is not hard to find. It is natural for us to be moved by the misfortunes of anyone who is our companion and fellow sufferer, because it seems to us we are threatened in the same way. So we are glad to lend a hand if we can, because to ignore these misfortunes would seem to us to be agreeing all too clearly deep down inside that the same may happen to us, given the right circumstances. Now scoundrels, who are in the majority in this world, and the richest people in it, think of all the other scoundrels, even if they do not even know them by sight, as their companions and fellow sufferers, and they feel obliged, by that league as it were, which as I have said exists between them, to help them in their need. Also, they think it a scandal that a man known to be a scoundrel should be seen to be in poor circumstances. The reason for this is that the world, which always honours virtue with words, is very likely in such cases to call poverty a punishment, and this is something that results in disgrace, and can turn out to be harmful, to all of them. They work so effectively to remove this scandal that, apart from people who are quite obscure, we see few examples of villains who, when they have fallen on hard times, do not by some means or other improve their circumstances until they are bearable.

The good and high-minded, on the contrary, since they are different from the majority, are regarded by the majority as creatures of another species. Consequently, they are not only not regarded as friends or fellow sufferers, but also not considered to be entitled to human rights. They are always seen to be persecuted more or less severely according to the degree of low-mindedness and the wickedness of the times and the people among whom they happen to live. Nature always tends to purge creatures' bodies of those humours and those active principles which do not sit well with the ones of which the bodies should rightly be composed, and Nature also brings it about in groups composed of many people that whoever differs very much from the generality, especially if such difference is so great as to be contrariety, should at all costs be destroyed or driven out. Also, the good and the high-minded are usually loathed because they tend to be sincere and call things by their proper names. This is a fault that the human race does not pardon, because it does not hate the evildoer, or evil itself, as much as it hates the person who calls it that. The result of this is that often, while the evildoer obtains riches, honours and power, he who names him is dragged to the scaffold, since people are very ready to suffer anything at the hands of others or at the will of Heaven, provided that they are said to be saved from it.

2

Run through the lives of famous men, and if you look at those who are such not merely by ascription, but by their actions, you will, despite all your efforts, find very few of the truly great who were not fatherless in their youth. I am not thinking of the fact that he whose father is alive (speaking of those who live on inherited income) is usually a man without means, and consequently can achieve nothing in the world, particularly when he is at the same time rich in expectations, so that he gives no thought to earning anything by his own effort, which might result in great deeds. (This is not a common circumstance, however, since generally those who have achieved great things have from the start been rich or at least well furnished with the world's goods.) Ignoring all this, a father's power, in all those nations that have laws, involves a sort of slavery for his sons. This slavery, because it is domestic, is more pressing and more perceptible than civil slavery. Although it may be moderated by the laws themselves, or by common custom, or by the personal qualities of the people involved, it never fails to produce a very damaging effect: that feeling which a man always has in his mind while his father lives, and which is bound to be confirmed by public opinion. I mean a feeling of subjection and dependence, of not being free and not being one's own master, indeed of not being, so to speak, a whole person, but merely a part and a member, a feeling that one's own name belongs more to someone else. This feeling is all the more profound in those more capable of action. Since they are more wide awake, they are more capable of feeling, and more shrewd to recognize the truth of their own condition. It is almost impossible that this feeling should go together with, I will not say doing, but planning anything great. And once his youth has gone by in this way, it hardly needs to be said that the man of forty or fifty who feels for the first time that he is his own master has no incentive, and, if he did have any, would have no enthusiasm or strength or time for great actions. So even in this matter it is clear that we can have nothing good in this world which is not accompanied by bad in equal measure. The inestimable value of having before one's eyes in one's youth an expert and loving guide, such as only one's own father can be, is offset by a sort of insignificance in youth and in life generally.

3

The economic wisdom of this century can be measured by what happens with the so-called "compact" editions, where there is little consumption of paper, and endless wear and tear on the eyesight. However, in defence of saving paper on books one might mention that it is the custom in this century to print much and read nothing. To this custom belongs also the abandonment of those round letters that were used generally in Europe in past centuries, and the substitution for them of long letters, to which we might add the gloss on the paper. These are things which are the more beautiful to look at the more harmful they are to the reader's eyes. But all this is very reasonable at a time when books are printed to be seen and not to be read.

4

What follows is not a thought, but a story, which I am telling here for the reader's amusement. A friend of mine, my life's companion in fact, Antonio Ranieri – a young man who, if he lives, and if people do not go so far as to render his natural gifts useless, will soon be

significant by the mere mention of his name – was living with me in
1831 in Florence. One summer evening, while he was walking along
Via Buia, he found many people standing on the corner near to the
Piazza del Duomo, under a ground-floor window of the building
which is now the Palazzo de' Riccardi. They were saying very fear-
fully, "Ah! The phantom!" And looking through the window into the
room, where there was no other light but that which came in from
one of the street lamps, he himself saw what looked like the shade of
a woman who was throwing her arms about but was otherwise quite
still. However, since he had other things on his mind, he passed on,
and during that evening and for the whole of the next day he forgot
that encounter. The next evening, at the same time, happening to
pass once more by the same place, he found that there was a larger
multitude there than the previous evening, and heard them repeating
with the same terror, "Ah! The phantom!" And looking through the
window, he saw the same shade, again throwing its arms about but
not making any other movement. The window was not much higher
than a man, and one of the crowd, who seemed to be a policeman,
said, "If someone would take me on his shoulders, I'd climb up and
see what's inside." To this Ranieri said, "If you hold me up, I'll do
the climbing." And when the other said, "Climb up," he did climb
up, placing his feet on the other's shoulders. He discovered, near to
the bars of the window, stretched out on the back of a chair, a black
apron which, when the wind stirred it, looked like arms waving about,
and on the chair, leaning against the back of it, a distaff which seemed
to be the head of the shade. Ranieri took the distaff in his hand and
showed it to the people, who dispersed, roaring with laughter.

What is the point of this little tale? It makes, as I have said, a
diversion for the reader, and I suspect also that it may even be not
entirely useless to historical criticism and to philosophy to know

that in the nineteenth century, in the very centre of Florence, which is the most cultured city in Italy, and where especially the people have most understanding and are most urbane, phantoms are seen, which are believed to be spirits and are in fact distaffs. And here foreigners must restrain their tendency to smile, as they like to do at our affairs, because it is well known that of the three great nations* which, as the papers say, "are at the forefront of civilization" none believes in spirits less than the Italians do.

5

In abstruse matters the minority always sees better than the majority, while the majority sees better in things that are evident. It is absurd in questions of metaphysics to bring into play what is called the general consensus, and no one attaches any importance to that consensus in physical matters, which are subject to the senses, as for example in the matter of the movement of the earth, and a thousand others. On the contrary, however, it is a thing which is foolhardy, dangerous and in the long run useless to oppose the opinion of the majority in civil affairs.

6

Death is not an evil, because it frees us from all evils, and while it takes away good things, it takes away also the desire for them. Old age is the supreme evil, because it deprives us of all pleasures, leaving us only the appetite for them, and it brings with it all sufferings. Nevertheless, we fear death, and we desire old age.

7

There is, strange to say, a disdain of death, a courage which is more abject and despicable than fear. That is the disdain of businessmen and others dedicated to making money, who very often, even for minimum gain, and for niggardly savings, obstinately neglect precautions and measures necessary for their own preservation, and put themselves in extreme danger, where not seldom, as contemptible heroes, they die a shameful death. There have been striking examples of this disgraceful courage, not without consequent harms and the massacre of innocent people, during the plague, which we like to call *cholera morbus*, a scourge of the human race in recent years.

8

One of the serious errors into which people fall every day is to believe that a secret of theirs is being kept. And not only the secret which they reveal in confidence, but even that which without their wish, or even against it, someone discovers or otherwise gets to know, and which they had rather were kept hidden. What I am saying is that you are mistaken every time when, aware that some business of yours is clearly known to someone else, you fail to be convinced that it is common knowledge, whatever harm or shame this may bring you. Having regard for their own best interests, people make a great effort not to reveal private things, but in what concerns other people no one stays silent. If you wish to verify this, look into yourself, and see how often you are restrained from revealing something you know by the displeasure or harm or shame that this might bring to someone else. I mean revealing it, if not to many people, at least to this or that friend, which comes to the same thing. In society there is nothing more needed than gossip, the main way of passing time, which is one of the first necessities of life. And no subject of gossip is more striking than one that arouses curiosity and banishes boredom, as new and secret things do. Therefore take this for a definite rule: whatever you do not wish to be known to have done, not only do not tell it, but do not do it. And whatever you cannot undo, or make as though it has never been, be sure that it is known, even if you do not notice.

9

No one who, against other people's opinion, has predicted the outcome of something exactly as it then turns out, should think that those who opposed him, once they see what has happened, will say he was right, and say he was wiser or more understanding than they were. No, they will deny the fact, or the prediction, or else they will allege that the circumstances differ somehow. Or they will find some other way to convince themselves and others that their opinion was correct, and the opposite opinion mistaken.

10

We know for certain that the majority of those whom we appoint to educate our children have not themselves been educated. And we should be in no doubt that they cannot give what they have not received, and what cannot be acquired in any other way.

11

There are some centuries which, in arts and studies (not to mention other matters), presume to remake everything, because they know how to make nothing.

12

He who with trouble and sufferings, or even only after waiting a long time, has achieved something desirable, if he sees another achieve the same thing easily and quickly, does not in fact lose anything he possesses. Nevertheless, such a thing is bound to be very hateful, because in the imagination the achievement diminishes out of all proportion if it is held in common with him who has expended or suffered little or nothing to obtain it. Therefore, in the parable, the workers in the vineyard complain of an injustice done to themselves, because a wage equal to theirs has been given to those who have done less work. Similarly, the brothers in certain religious orders are accustomed to treat their novices with every kind of harshness, for fear they will without any effort reach that state which they themselves only attained after some discomfort.

13

It is a pleasant and attractive illusion that the anniversary of an event (which has really no more to do with it than with any other day of the year) seems to have a particular connection with the event, as if a shadow from the past always rises again and returns on those days, and stands before us. This is some cure for the sad thought of the annihilation of what has been, and some comfort for the grief we feel for many losses, because those recurrences seem to suggest that what is past, and never returns, is not quite dead and gone. This is like finding ourselves in places where things have happened which are memorable either in themselves or on our account, and saying that this happened here, and here this, and believing we are, so to speak, nearer to those events than when we find ourselves elsewhere. So when we say that a year ago today or so many years ago such a thing happened, or something else happened, this event seems to us, so to speak, more present, or less past, than on other days. And this fancy is so deeply rooted in mankind that it seems hard for us to believe that the anniversary is as alien to the event itself as any other day is. This is why the annual celebration of important memories, religious as well as civil, public as well as private, birthdays and days of death of people who are dear to us, and suchlike, was and is common to all nations that have, or had, memories and a calendar. And I have noticed, having asked several people about it, that sensitive people, used to solitude or to internal conversations, are usually very diligent in keeping anniversaries, and live, so to speak, on remembrances of this kind, always going over them, and saying to themselves that on a day of the year like the present this or that thing happened to them.

14

It would be no small unhappiness to educators, and above all to parents, if they were to think what is most true: that their children, whatever disposition they may have been endowed with, and whatever effort, diligence and expense may have gone into educating them, with subsequent experience of the world, almost without doubt, if death does not prevent them, will become wicked. This would perhaps make a sounder and more reasonable reply than that given by Thales. Asked by Solon why he was not married, he replied by showing how parents worry over the misfortunes and dangers of their children. It would, in my opinion, be sounder and more reasonable to excuse oneself by saying that one did not want to increase the number of the wicked.

15

Chilon, who is numbered among the Seven Sages of Greece, advised that the man who is physically strong should be gentle in his behaviour, with the purpose, he said, of inspiring in others reverence rather than fear. Affability, a pleasant manner and even humility are never superfluous in those who, in beauty or intellect or in anything else much desired by the world, are manifestly superior to the majority. This is because the fault for which they have to beg pardon is so grievous, and the enemy they have to placate is so cruel and exacting. The former is superiority, and the latter is envy. The ancients believed this. When they found themselves honoured and in prosperity, they thought it necessary to placate the very gods, expiating with humiliation, with offerings and with voluntary penances the scarcely expiable sin of happiness and excellence.

16

If, as the Emperor Otho says according to Tacitus, the guilty and the innocent have the same end prepared for them, then it is a more human thing to deserve one's fate. This opinion is not very different, I believe, from that of those who, having lofty minds and being naturally disposed to virtue, once they have gone into the world and experienced the ingratitude, the injustice and the disgraceful fury of men against their fellows (and even more against the virtuous), embrace wickedness, and do this not through corruption, or drawn by example, as the weak are, or even out of self-interest, or through too great a desire for base and trifling human benefits, or ultimately in the hope of saving themselves in the general wickedness, but by their free choice, and to avenge themselves on men, and pay them back in their own coin, taking up their own arms against them. The wickedness of such people is all the more profound as it is born out of experience of virtue, and it is all the more formidable insofar as it is joined (no ordinary thing) to greatness and strength of mind, and is a sort of heroism.

17

As the prisons and galleys are full of people who are, according to themselves, completely innocent, so public offices and positions of every kind are held only by people called to them and compelled to accept them very much against their will. It is almost impossible to find anyone who admits either to having merited the punishments he suffers, or sought the responsibilities he enjoys. Perhaps, however, the latter is less likely than the former.

18

I saw a man in Florence dragging along, like a draught animal, as the custom is there, a cart full of goods. He walked with the greatest of arrogance, shouting and commanding people to get out of his way. And he seemed to me a symbol of many who walk full of pride, insulting others, for reasons not dissimilar to what caused his arrogance – that is, pulling a cart.

19

There are some few people in the world condemned to have little success in any dealings with others because – not through inexperience or ignorance of social life, but through their own invariable cast of mind

– they cannot rid themselves of a certain simplicity of behaviour, devoid of those rather deceptive and artificial appearances, which all others (including fools), even if they never realize it, always have at their disposal and make use of, and which in them, and in their own eyes, is very difficult to distinguish from what is natural. These people of whom I speak, since they are obviously different from others, being regarded as incapable of coping with worldly matters, are despised and badly treated even by their inferiors, and seldom listened to or obeyed by their dependants, because they all think themselves above them and look down on them. Everyone who has anything to do with them tries to deceive them and take advantage of them more than he would anyone else, believing this is easier and can be done with impunity. So from all sides faith is not kept with them; they are abused, and what is just and right is denied them. Wherever there is competition, they are overcome, even by those who are very inferior to them, not only in their mental powers or other intrinsic qualities, but in those which the world recognizes and appreciates more, like beauty, youth, strength, courage and even wealth. Finally, whatever their station in life, they cannot get the same degree of consideration as greengrocers and porters. That is reasonable in a way, because it is no small innate defect or disadvantage not to be able, despite all their efforts, to learn what even dolts learn easily – that is, that art which alone makes men and boys look like men. After all, such people, despite being naturally inclined to goodness, and being better acquainted with men and life than many others, are in no way, as they sometimes seem to be, better than we are allowed to be without having to be ashamed of it. And they lack the manners current in the world, not through goodness or by their own choice, but because they have not been able to learn them, despite all their zeal and study. The result is that nothing remains for them but to adapt their minds to their condition, and to be careful above all not to try to hide or dissimulate that frankness and that natural way of behaving which is their own, because nothing is so bad or so ridiculous as when they affect the usual affectation of others.

20

If I had Cervantes's talent, I would write a book to purge – as he purged Spain of the imitation of knights errant – Italy, indeed the civilized world, of a vice which, considering the mildness of current manners, and perhaps even without that consideration, is no less cruel and barbarous than any remnant of medieval savagery castigated by Cervantes. I mean the vice of reading or performing one's own compositions in front of others. This is an ancient vice, which was tolerable in previous centuries because it was rare, but which today, when everyone writes and it is very difficult to find someone who is not an author, has become a scourge, a public calamity, one further tribulation for human beings. And it is not a joke but the simple truth to say that, on account of this, acquaintances are suspect and friendships dangerous, and that there is no time or place where an innocent person does not have to fear being assaulted, and subjected on the very spot, or after being dragged elsewhere, to the torture of hearing endless prose or thousands of lines of verse, no longer with the excuse of wanting to learn his opinion – an excuse which for a long time it was customary to give as the reason for such performances – but solely and expressly to give pleasure to the author by hearing them, apart from the inevitable praise at the end. In all conscience I believe that on the one hand the childishness of human nature, and the extremity of blindness, indeed of stupidity, to which man is led by his *amour propre*, and on the other hand how far we can deceive ourselves, are shown in few things more clearly than in this matter of reciting one's own writings. Because, while everyone is himself fully aware of the unspeakable annoyance he always feels when he hears other people's writings, and everyone sees people whom he invites to listen to his writings shudder and grow pale and adduce all sorts of obstacles to excuse themselves, and even run away and hide as well as they can, nevertheless, brazen-faced and amazingly persevering, like a hungry bear, he searches out and pursues his prey through the whole city, and once he has caught up with it, drags it to the destined place. And during the performance, although he is aware, first by the yawning, then by the stretching and writhing, and by a hundred other signs, of the mortal anguish felt by the unhappy listener, this does not make him stop or pause. Indeed, he gets fiercer and fiercer and more dogged, and goes on haranguing and shouting for hours, in fact for whole days and nights almost, until he becomes hoarse, and until, long after his listener has fainted, he feels his own strength is exhausted, although he is still not satisfied. During this time, while the man slaughters his neighbour, it is certain that he experiences an almost superhuman and paradisal pleasure, since we see that people forsake every other pleasure for this one, and forget their food and sleep, while life and the world disappear from their vision. And this pleasure consists of the firm belief that the man has in arousing admiration and giving pleasure to whomever hears him. If this were not so, it would be all the same to him if he recited to the desert rather than to people. Now, as I have said, everyone knows by experience what pleasure the hearer has (I always say hearer and not listener advisedly), and the performer can see it. And I know also that many would choose great physical suffering in preference to a pleasure like this. Even the most beautiful and valuable writings, when their own author is reciting them, become such as to kill with boredom. In this connection a philologist friend of mine has observed that, if it is true that Octavia fainted when she heard Virgil read the sixth book of the *Aeneid*, we may well believe that that happened not so much because she was reminded of her son Marcellus, as they say, as through boredom on hearing the reading.

Such is man. And this vice of which I am speaking, which is so barbarous and ridiculous, and contrary to the good sense of a rational creature, is truly an illness endemic to the human race, because there is no nation so noble, nor any kind of people, nor any period, in which this plague is not found. Italians, French, English, Germans; white-haired men, very wise in other things, full of intellect and worth; men well experienced in the ways of society, with very polite manners, who love to observe foolishness and make fun of it; all of these turn into cruel children when it is a matter of reading out their own compositions. And just as this is a vice of our time, so it was in the time of Horace, to whom already it seemed unbearable. So it was also in the time of Martial who, when he was asked by someone why he did not read his verses to him, replied, "So as not to hear yours." And so it was also in the greatest age of Greece when, we are told, Diogenes the Cynic, finding himself in a company where everyone was dying of boredom at one such reading, and seeing at the end of the book, which was in the author's hands, a blank page appear, said, "Take heart, friends. I see land ahead."

But today the thing has come to such a pitch that the number of hearers, even under compulsion, can hardly meet the authors' needs. Some of my acquaintances, therefore, hard-working men, having considered this point, and being convinced that the recitation of one's own works is a human need, have thought of making provision for it, and at the same time turning it, as all public needs are turned, to a particular use. For this purpose they will shortly be opening a school or academy, or rather an Institute of Listening where, at any hour of the day or night, they, or people paid by them, will listen to whoever wishes to read, at set prices, as follows: for prose, for the first hour, one *scudo*, the second hour two *scudi*, the third hour four *scudi*, the fourth hour eight, and so on in geometrical progression. Poetry will cost double. For every passage read, if the reader wishes to read it again, as does happen, one *lira* a line. If the listener falls asleep, the reader will be reimbursed with a third of the price. For convulsions, fainting fits and other accidents, slight or serious, which may happen to one party or the other in the course of the reading, the school will be supplied with essences and medicines that will be dispensed free. So, by making a profit from something that up to now has yielded no dividend (I mean our ears), a new road will be opened up for industry, with an increase of the general wealth.

21

We do not feel any lively and lasting pleasure in conversation, except insofar as we are allowed to talk about ourselves, and of the things which occupy us, or which relate to us in some way. Any other talk soon starts to bore us, and whatever pleases us is deadly boring to the listener. No one is regarded as amiable except at the price of suffering, because in conversation only he is amiable who gratifies others' *amour propre*, first by listening a lot and staying silent a lot, something which is usually very tedious, then by letting others talk about themselves and their own affairs for as long as they wish, in fact encouraging them in such dissertations, and by himself talking about such things. The result is that they go away very pleased with themselves, and he goes away dreadfully bored by them. Because, in short, if the best companions are those from whom we go away more pleased with ourselves, it more or less follows that they are those whom we leave more bored. The conclusion must be that in conversations and in any discussion where the intention is only to amuse ourselves by talking, almost inevitably some people's pleasure is other people's boredom, and one can hope for nothing but to be either bored or to displease, and one is very fortunate if one is able to have equal experience of both.

22

It is in my opinion very difficult to decide whether it is more contrary to the basic principles of good breeding to be in the habit of talking about oneself at length, or whether it is rarer to find someone without this vice.

23

The common saying that life is a theatrical performance is verified above all in this: that the world constantly speaks in one way, and just as constantly acts in another. Since nowadays all are actors in this comedy, because they all talk in the same way, and practically no one is a spectator, because the empty language of the world deceives only children and fools, it follows that this performance has become something completely inept, an effort that is boring and pointless. It would therefore be an undertaking worthy of our century finally to make life not a simulated action but a true one, and to overcome for the first time in the history of the world the notorious discrepancy between words and deeds. Since our actions are by now known by experience to be unchangeable, and it is not right that men should tire themselves out any longer looking for the impossible, this reconciliation has to be achieved by that means which is the only one and at the same time very easy, although up to now it has not been tried, and this is to change the words, and for once call things by their proper names.

24

Unless I am deceived, it is a rare thing in our century to find someone generally praised whose praises have not originated from his own mouth. Egoism is so powerful, and the envy and hatred which men have towards one another so great, that if you want to get a name, it is not enough to perform praiseworthy actions. You must praise them or, what amounts to the same thing, find someone who will continually recommend them and extol them for you, singing your praises loudly in the ears of the public, constraining people both by example and by zealous perseverance to repeat some of those praises. Do not hope that they will say one word spontaneously, whatever greatness and worth you show, however fine the works which you achieve. They gaze and remain silent for ever. If they can, they prevent others seeing. Whoever wishes to rise, even by genuine merit, must banish modesty. In this respect also the world is like women, for we get nothing from it by modesty and reserve.

25

No one is so completely disillusioned with the world, or acquainted so thoroughly with it, or has such hatred for it, that if it regards him benignly for a while, he does not feel somewhat reconciled to it. Similarly, no one is known by us to be so wicked that if he greets us courteously he does not seem to us less wicked than he was. These observations serve to demonstrate the weakness of mankind, not to justify the wicked or the world.

26

The man who is inexperienced in the ways of the world, and often also he who is not inexperienced, in the first instant when he realizes he has been struck by some disaster, particularly when it is not his fault, if friends and relatives come into his mind, or people in general, he does not expect from them anything other than commiseration and comfort, to say nothing of help, and that they will have either more love or more regard for him than before. Nothing is further from his mind than to see himself, because of his misfortune, socially degraded almost, seen by the eyes of the world as guilty of some misdeed, fallen into disgrace among his friends, with his friends and acquaintances on all sides in flight, and then from a distance delighting in his misfortune and holding him in derision. Similarly, if he has some good fortune, one of the first thoughts that comes to him is that he must share his joy with his friends, and that perhaps they will turn out to be even more pleased at his good fortune than he is himself. It does not occur to him that, on the announcement of his good luck, the faces of his dear ones will be contorted and darken. Some will be dismayed. Many will at first try hard not to believe it, and then to lessen in his and their own and others' estimation his recent good fortune. In certain people, because of this, friendship will cool, and in others turn to hatred. Finally, not a few will do all that is in their power to deprive him of his good fortune. So the imagination and the ideas of mankind are innately distant from and abhor the reality of life.

27

There is no clearer sign of not being very philosophical or wise than wishing all life to be wise and philosophical.

28

The human race, or any least portion of it beyond the single individual, divides into two groups: the ones who bully, and the others who suffer their bullying. Since neither laws nor force, nor any progress in philosophy or civilization can prevent any man born or about to be born from being one or the other, all that remains is, for him who can choose, to choose. Certainly not everyone can, or not always.

29

No profession is so sterile as that of letters. However, so great is the value of imposture in the world, that with its help even letters become fruitful. Imposture is the soul, so to speak, of social life, and the art without which indeed no art and no faculty, considered with regard to its effect on human minds, is perfect. Whenever you look into the fortunes of two people, the one of true worth in any sphere and the other whose worth is false, you will find that the latter is more successful than the former. Indeed, most often the latter is fortunate, and the former unfortunate. Imposture is valid and efficacious even without the truth, but without it the truth can do nothing. And that does not come, in my opinion, from the evil inclination of our race, but because the truth is always too poor and inadequate, so that men always need, if they are to be delighted or moved, some illusion and sleight of hand. They must be promised something much bigger and better than can be given. Nature herself is an impostor towards man, making his life lovable and endurable principally by means of imagination and deception.

30

As humankind is in the habit of upbraiding present things, and praising those which are past, so most travellers, while they are travelling, love their native place and somewhat angrily prefer it to wherever they find themselves. Having returned to their native place, with the same anger they value it less than all the other places where they have been.

31

In every land the universal vices and ills of mankind and of human society are noted as peculiar to that place. I have never been anywhere where I have not heard, "Here the women are vain and inconstant; they read little and they're poorly educated. Here the public are curious about other people's affairs, and they're very talkative and slanderous. Here money, favour and baseness can achieve anything. Here envy rules, and friendships are hardly sincere," and so on and so on, as if things went on differently elsewhere. Men are wretched by necessity, and determined to believe themselves wretched by accident.

32

As he advances every day in his practical knowledge of life, a man loses some of that severity which makes it difficult for young people, always looking for perfection, and expecting to find it, and judging everything by that idea of it which they have in their minds, to pardon defects and concede that there is some value in virtues that are poor and inadequate, and in good qualities that are unimportant, when they happen to find them in people. Then, seeing how everything is imperfect, and being convinced that there is nothing better in the world than that small good which they despise, and that practically nothing or no one is truly estimable, little by little, altering their standards and comparing what they come across not with perfection any more, but with reality, they grow accustomed to pardoning freely and valuing every mediocre virtue, every shadow of worth, every least ability that they find. So much so that, ultimately, many things and many people seem to them praiseworthy that at first would have seemed to them scarcely endurable. This goes so far that, whereas initially they hardly had the ability to feel esteem, in the course of time they become almost unable to despise. And this to a greater extent the more intelligent they are. Because in fact to be very contemptuous and discontented, once our first youth is past, is not a good sign, and those who are such cannot, either because of the poverty of their intellects or because they have little experience, have been much acquainted with the world. Or else they are among those fools who despise others because of the great esteem in which they hold themselves. In short, it seems hardly probable, but it is true, and it indicates only the extreme baseness of human affairs to say it, that experience of the world teaches us to appreciate rather than to depreciate.

33

Mediocre deceivers, and women generally, always believe that their tricks have worked, and that people have been caught out by them. Those who are more astute, however, doubt this, being better acquainted on the one hand with the difficulties of the art, and on the other with its power, and knowing that their wish to deceive is everyone's wish, which means that often the deceiver turns out to be deceived. Besides this, the more astute do not think others have so little understanding as they are imagined to have by those who understand little themselves.

34

Young men very commonly believe that they make themselves likeable by pretending to be melancholy. And perhaps, when it is feigned, melancholy can for a short time be pleasing, especially to women. But true melancholy is shunned by the whole of humankind, and in the long run nothing pleases and nothing is successful in our dealings with people but cheerfulness. Because ultimately, contrary to what young men think, the world, quite rightly, does not like to weep, but to laugh.

35

Occasionally in places that are half civilized and half barbarous, as for example Naples, something is more noticeable than it is elsewhere, although it happens everywhere in one way or another – that is, that the man who is reputed to be penniless is regarded as hardly a man, while the man who is reputed to be moneyed is always in danger of his life. This is the reason why people generally act as they do there, as they have to in such places. They decide to make their own financial state a mystery so that the public will not know whether to despise them or to murder them. So one should only be as men ordinarily are, half despised and half esteemed, at times in danger of harm and at times left alone.

36

Many want to act meanly towards you, and at the same time want you, on pain of their hatred, to be careful on the one hand not to obstruct their meanness, and on the other hand not to see them as mean.

37

No human quality is more intolerable in ordinary life, or in fact tolerated less, than intolerance.

38

As the art of fencing is useless when the fight is between two fencers of equal skill, because neither has any greater advantage over the other than if they were both unskilled, so it very often happens that men are false and wicked without gaining anything by it, because they encounter each other with equal wickedness and dissimulation, in such a way that the matter ends as it would do if both had been sincere and honest. There is no doubt that, in the last analysis, wickedness and duplicity are only useful when they are allied with force, or when they come across a lesser wickedness or shrewdness, or rather when they come across goodness. This last case is rare; the second (insofar as it concerns wickedness) is not common, because the majority of people are wicked in the same way, more or less. And so one can hardly overestimate how frequently they could, by acting well towards each other, obtain the same result with ease which they now obtain with a great effort, or even do not obtain, by doing, or trying hard to do, evil.

39

Baldassarre Castiglione in *The Book of the Courtier* very helpfully gives the reason why old people are in the habit of praising the time when they were young and upbraiding the present time. He says, "So the reason for this false notion which old people have is, I think, that the years, as they flee away, take with them many comforts, and among these they take most of the vital spirits from the blood, so that our temperament changes, and the organs by means of which the soul exercises its powers become feeble. And so, as the leaves fall from the trees in autumn, from our hearts at that time fall the sweet flowers of contentment, and in place of serene and clear thoughts cloudy and troubled sadness enters, accompanied by a thousand calamities. The result is that not only is the body weak, but the mind is weak too, and of past pleasures it preserves only a tenacious memory, and the image of that dear time of our tender age – in which when we find ourselves again, it seems to us that heaven and earth and all things are always celebrating a festival and everything is smiling on us all round, and in our thoughts, as in a delightful and beautiful garden, the sweet spring of cheerfulness blooms. And so, when the sun of our life in the cold season is already beginning to depart towards its setting, despoiling us of those pleasures, it would perhaps be help-ful if we were to lose not only them, but the memory of them, and find, as Themistocles has it, an art which teaches us to forget. Our bodily senses are so fallible that often they deceive the judgement of the mind. And so in my opinion old people are like those who, as they are leaving the port, keep their eyes cast down, so that it seems to them that the ship is immobile and the shore is moving away. Of course the contrary is the case, for the port, like the time we dream of and its pleasures, remains where it was, and we, fleeing with the ship of mortality, depart one after another on that stormy sea which absorbs and devours everything. Nor are we ever allowed to make landfall again. Instead, after being buffeted continually by contrary winds, we are shipwrecked on a reef. And so, the aged mind being inadequate to cope with many pleasures, it cannot relish them. Just as to those suffering from a fever, when their palates have been spoilt by corrupt vapours, all wines seem bitter, however precious and exquisite they may be, so to old people because of their indisposition (although they do not lack desire) pleasures seem insipid and cold and very different from those which they remember enjoying, although the pleasures in themselves remain as they were. And so, feeling themselves deprived, they complain, and upbraid the present age as wicked, not realizing that it is they themselves who have changed and not the times. And, on the contrary, calling past pleasures to mind, they call back to mind also the time in which they enjoyed those pleasures, and so they praise that time as good, because it seems to bring with it a hint of what they felt when it was present. In effect our minds hate all things associated with our troubles and love those associated with our pleasures."

Thus Castiglione, expounding in a manner that is no less beautiful than florid, as was the custom with our Italian prose writers, a great truth. In confirmation of it, one may mention that old people prefer the past to the present not only in things which depend on mankind, but also in those which do not, accusing them likewise of having deteriorated, not so much in old people and in relation to them (which is true), but generally and in themselves. I believe everyone remembers having heard many times from his elders (as I remember hearing from mine) that the years have become colder than they were, and the winters longer, and that, in their day, around Easter they used to leave off their winter clothes and put on their summer things, which today, according to them, can hardly be done in May, or even at times in June. And not many years ago, the cause of this supposed cooling of the seasons was investigated seriously by some physicists. The deforestation of the mountains was suggested, and I know not what else, to explain something which did not happen. Indeed the opposite is the case. Someone has observed for example that, judging by various passages in ancient authors, in Roman times Italy must have been colder than it is now. This is also very easy to believe because it is clear from experience, and from natural causes, that the progress of human civilization renders the air, in inhabited lands, milder day by day. This effect has been, and is, especially obvious in America, where within our memory a mature civilization has succeeded a state of barbarism in some parts, and mere solitude in other parts. But old people, since the cold troubles them much more at their present age than it did in their youth, believe that the change which they experience in their own condition has happened outside them, and imagine that the heat which is diminishing in them is diminishing in the air and on the earth. This fancy is so well established that exactly what our old people affirm to us was already affirmed by, to go no further back, the old people of a century and a half ago to the contemporaries of Magalotti, who wrote in his *Familiar Letters*: "It certainly seems that the ancient order of the seasons is being perverted. Here in Italy there is a common opinion and complaint that the turns of the seasons no longer exist, and that in this blurring of the boundaries there is no doubt that cold is gaining ground. I have heard my father say that, in his youth in Rome, on the morning of Easter Sunday everyone put on summer clothes. Now anyone who does not have to pawn his shirt takes good care, I can tell you, not to leave off the lightest garment of those which he was wearing in the depths of winter."

That is what Magalotti wrote in the year 1683. Italy would by now be colder than Greenland if from that year to this it had continued to cool at the rate which he mentions. It is hardly necessary to add that the continuous cooling which is said to occur from causes intrinsic to the mass of the earth has no bearing on the present subject, since it is something which, because of its slowness, is not perceptible in tens of centuries, much less in a few years.

40

It is very undesirable to speak a great deal about oneself. But young people, when they have lively natures, and their spirits are raised above the common level, are the less able to keep themselves free from this vice. And they speak of their own affairs with extreme candour, taking it for granted that the listener is only a little less interested than they are themselves. And they are pardoned for doing this, not so much in consideration of their inexperience, as because of the clear need they have of help, counsel and a verbal outlet for the passions which disturb them at their age. And also it seems to be generally recognized that young people have a kind of right to want the world to be occupied with their thoughts.

41

We are seldom right to consider ourselves offended by things said about us in our absence or with no intention that they should come to our ears. Because if we try to remember and examine carefully our own habits, we find we have no friend so dear, and hold no one in such veneration, that it would not greatly displease them to hear many of the words and the conversations which come from our mouths about them in their absence. On the one hand, our *amour propre* is so excessively sensitive, and so captious, that it is almost impossible that one word said about us in our absence, if it is faithfully reported to us, should not seem to us unworthy or hardly worthy of us, and not sting us. On the other hand, it is hard to exaggerate how contrary our practice is to the precept not to do unto others what we would not want them to do unto us, and how much freedom we allow ourselves in speaking about other people.

<h1 style="text-align:center">42</h1>

It is a curious feeling for the man of little more than twenty-five years of age when, apparently all of a sudden, he realizes that many of his companions consider him more mature than they are, and he notices on reflection that there are in fact many people in the world younger than he is, when he is accustomed to think of himself as, beyond dispute, in the flower of his youth, and even if he is thought to be inferior to the others in everything, to believe himself not excelled by anyone in youth. This is because those younger than he is, still little more than boys, and seldom his companions, have not formed part, so to speak, of his world. Then he starts to feel how the merit of youth, regarded by him as almost part of his essential nature, so much so that it would have been scarcely possible for him to imagine himself apart from it, has only been given for a time, and he becomes anxious for such merit, both as a thing in itself and with regard to the opinion of others. It is certainly true – of no one who has passed the age of twenty-five, after which the bloom of youth immediately starts to fade, can one truly say, except of someone who is stupid – that he has no experience of misfortune. This is because, even if fate had been propitious to someone in every way, he would still, once he had passed that stage, be conscious in himself of a misfortune graver and bitterer than any other, and perhaps graver and bitterer to one who in other respects had been less unfortunate – the decline and fall of his precious youth.

43

In this world, it is those men who are remarkable for their integrity from whom, if you are on friendly terms with them, you can, although not hoping for any service, not fear any disservice.

44

If you question the subordinates of any official or government minister about his qualities and his conduct, particularly in his official capacity, even if their replies agree about the facts, you will find great disagreement over the interpretation of them. And even if their interpretations agree, their judgements will vary endlessly, some people blaming what others exalt. It is only with regard to his abstention – or otherwise – from other people's goods or public property that you will not find two people who, agreeing on the facts, disagree either in interpreting them or in judging them, and who, with one voice, will not simply praise the official for his abstinence, or condemn him for the contrary. In short, it appears that good and bad officials are known and assessed by nothing other than this question of money. In fact, a good official is one who is self-denying, a bad official is one who is greedy. This means that a public officer can in his own way dispose of the life, the honesty and everything else citizens have, and will not only be excused for all of his actions but praised, provided he does not touch their money. It is as if people, disagreeing in their opinions over everything else, agree only in their respect for cash, or as if essentially money is the man, and nothing but money. This is something which really seems, from a thousand indications, to be regarded by the human race as an unvarying axiom, particularly in our time. In this connection a French philosopher of the last century used to say: "Ancient politicians always talked about morality and virtue, while modern politicians talk about nothing but commerce and cash."

According to some students of political economy, or pupils of philosophical newspapers, there is good reason for this, because virtue and morality, they say, cannot stand firm without the foundation of industry. Industry, by providing for daily necessities, and making life comfortable and secure for all classes of people, will make virtue stable and common to all. This is all very well. Together with industry, at the same time low-mindedness, coldness, egoism, avarice, falsity and treachery in commerce, all the qualities and passions which are most depraved and unworthy of civilized men, are in full vigour, and multiply endlessly. And we are still waiting for virtue.

45

The great remedy for slander, just as for troubles in the mind, is time. If the world condemns some projects or courses of ours, whether they be good or bad, we need to do nothing but persevere. After a little while, when the subject has become stale, the slanderers will abandon it in order to look for fresh subjects. And the firmer and more imperturbable we show ourselves as we carry on, and scorn what people say, the sooner what was, in the beginning, condemned or perceived as strange will be regarded as reasonable and normal. This is because the world, which never believes anyone wrong if he does not give in, eventually condemns itself, and absolves us. This is the reason why, as is often noted, the weak live according to the will of the world, and the strong according to their own will.

46

It does not do much credit, I do not know whether to men or to virtue, to notice that in all civilized tongues, ancient and modern, the same words signify goodness and stupidity; a worthy man or a man of little worth. Several words of this kind – such as *dabbenaggine* in Italian and *euethes*, *euetheia* in Greek,* without their proper meaning, which would perhaps not be very useful – either keep, or had from the beginning, only their pejorative meaning. This shows in how much esteem goodness has in all ages been held by the crowd, whose judgements and intimate feelings are clear, even at times despite themselves, in the forms of language. It is the constant judgement of the crowd, always dissimulated, since the very language they use is contradicted by how they talk, that no one who has the choice chooses to be good. Fools are good because they cannot be anything else.

47

Man is condemned either to consume his youth (which is the only time to store up fruit for the years to come and make provision for himself) without a purpose, or to waste it in procuring enjoyments for that part of his life in which he will no longer be capable of enjoyment.

48

We can measure the great love that nature gives us for our fellow beings by what any animal does if, like an inexperienced boy, it happens to see its own image in a mirror. Believing it to be a creature like itself, it flies into a rage and a frenzy, and tries in every way to harm that creature and to murder it. Domestic birds, tame as they are by nature and by habit, thrust themselves angrily at the mirror, screeching, with their wings stretched and their beaks open, and strike at it. Monkeys, when they can, throw it to the ground and grind it underfoot.

49

Creatures naturally hate their fellow creatures, and whenever their own interest requires it, harm them. We cannot therefore avoid hatred and injuries from men, while to a great extent we can avoid their scorn. This is why there is usually little point in the respect which young people and those new to the world pay to those they come across, not through mean-spiritedness or any other form of self-interest, but through a benevolent desire not to provoke enmity and to win hearts. They do not fulfil this desire, and in some ways they harm their own repute, because the person who is so respected comes to have a greater idea of himself, and he who pays the respect a lesser idea of himself. He who does not look to men for usefulness or fame, should not look for love either, since he will not obtain it. If he wants my opinion, he should preserve his own dignity completely, giving to everyone no more than his due. Thus he will be somewhat more hated and persecuted than otherwise, but not often despised.

50

The Jews have a book of precepts and various sayings translated, so they say, from the Arabic, but more likely, according to some, to be a purely Jewish composition. In it, among many other things of no importance, we read that a certain wise man, when someone said to him, "I love you," replied, "Why not, if you are not of my religion, or a relative of mine, or a neighbour, or someone who looks after me?" Our hatred of those who are like us is greater towards those who are most like us. Young people are, for a thousand and one reasons, more disposed to be friendly than other people are. Nevertheless, a lasting friendship is almost impossible between two men who lead the same youthful life. I mean the sort of life which goes under that name today, that is, one dedicated mainly to women. Indeed, between those two it is less possible than ever because of the vehemence of their passions, and their rivalry in love and the jealousies which inevitably arise between them, and because, as Madame de Staël has observed, another person's successes with women always displease even the greatest friend of the lucky man. Women are, after money, the thing in which men are least amenable and least capable of agreement, and where acquaintances, friends and brothers change their usual demeanour and nature. This is because men are friends and relatives, indeed civilized, and truly men, not up to the altar, as the old proverb has it, but up to the point of money and women, after which they become savage beasts. And in matters to do with women, although the inhumanity is less than in money matters, the envy is greater, because vanity is more involved – or rather, to put it better, *amour propre* is involved, the most characteristic and most sensitive of our loves. And we never see anyone smile or say sweet words to a woman (something we all do on occasion) without all those who are present trying, either outwardly or just within themselves, to deride him bitterly. So, although half the pleasure in successes of this kind, as also usually in other kinds, consists in recounting them, the revelation which young men make of their amorous joys is completely out of place, especially with other young men, because no subject was ever more disagreeable to anyone. Often, even when they are telling the truth, they are mocked.

51

When we see how seldom men are guided in their actions by a true judgement of what can help or harm them, we realize how easily anyone can be deceived who, with the intention of divining some secret decision, looks carefully to see what would be most useful either to him or to those by whom the decision is to be made. Guicciardini, speaking at the start of his seventeenth book about the discussion over what decisions Francis I of France would make after his liberation of the fortress of Madrid, says, "Perhaps those who talked in this way considered what he ought to do by the light of reason, rather than the nature of the French and how prudent they were. This is certainly an error into which we often fall in discussions and judgements concerning the disposition and will of others."* Guicciardini is perhaps the only historian among the moderns who understood men very well, and philosophized about events drawing on his knowledge of human nature, rather than on a certain political science – divorced from the study of man, and usually unreal – commonly employed by those historians, especially European and American, who have wished to reflect upon the facts, not contenting themselves, as most do, with recounting them in order and not thinking any further.

52

No one should think he has learnt how to live unless he has learnt to regard as a mere breath of wind any offers made to him by anyone, particularly the most spontaneous ones, however solemn they are and however often they may be repeated. And not only the offers which many people make, but their urgent and endless requests that others should take advantage of their skills. They specify the means and the circumstances of the matter, and they show very reasonably how the difficulties can be removed. The result is that if in the end, either persuaded, or perhaps overcome by the tedium of such requests, or for some other reason, you bring yourself to reveal to someone like this what you need, you will see him immediately grow pale, and then change the subject, or answer in only the vaguest of terms, leaving you quite dissatisfied. And after that, for a long time, you will be very lucky if, after much effort, you are allowed to see him again, or if, after you have brought yourself to his attention again by writing, you get a reply. People do not want to confer benefits because of the trouble it would cost them, and because the needs and misfortunes of their acquaintances never fail to give them some pleasure. But they like to be known as benefactors, and they like gratitude, together with that feeling of superiority which comes with being a benefactor. And so they offer what they do not wish to give. And the more reluctant they see you are, the more they insist, primarily to humiliate you and make you blush, but also because they have so much less fear that you will accept their offers. And so most courageously they thrust themselves forward to the last, scorning the ever-present danger that they will be shown up as impostors, and hoping that they will receive nothing but thanks, until at the first word of a request they turn in flight.

53

The ancient philosopher Bion used to say, "It is impossible to please the crowd, unless you become a hotchpotch, or a sweetened wine." But, if the present state of human society lasts, this impossibility will always be pursued, even by those who say, and also at times believe, they are not pursuing it, just as, so long as our species lasts, even those who know the human condition best will persevere until death looking for happiness, and promising it to themselves.

54

Take it as axiomatic that human beings, within themselves and away from everyone else, never stop, except briefly, believing true, against all evidence to the contrary, those things which are necessary to their peace of mind and, as it were, their ability to live. The old man, especially one who moves in society, to the end of his days never stops believing deep down inside (although he always protests the opposite) that he can, by a remarkable exception to the general rule, in some way which is unknown and inexplicable even to himself, still make some impression on women. That is because his condition would be altogether too wretched if he were completely convinced that he was excluded, utterly and for ever, from that good which the civilized man, in one way or another, and deluding himself more or less, ultimately comes to see as the purpose of life. The licentious woman, although she can see all day a thousand and one signs of the public's opinion of her, firmly believes that most people think her chaste, and that only a few of her old and new confidantes (few, I mean, in comparison with the public) know, and keep concealed from the world, and even from each other, the truth about her. The man whose conduct is mean and who, because of that very meanness and his lack of courage, is anxious about other people's opinion, believes that his actions are interpreted for the best, and that their true motives are not understood. It is similar with material things. Buffon observes that the sick man at the point of death does not really give any credence to his doctors or his friends, but only to his inmost hope, which promises an escape from the present danger.* I need hardly mention the astounding credulity and incredulity of husbands with regard to their wives, which is the subject of tales, scenes, raillery and continual laughter in those nations where matrimony is irrevocable. And so on and so forth. There is nothing in the world so false and so absurd that it is not believed to be true by very sensible people, whenever their minds cannot find any way of coming to terms with the opposite and being at peace with it. I am not forgetting that old people are less disposed than youngsters to stop believing what suits them, and to accept those beliefs which upset them. This is because youngsters have more strength of mind to face evil things, and a greater aptitude either to endure the consciousness of them or to be destroyed by them.

55

A woman is laughed at if she weeps in all sincerity for her dead husband, but severely blamed if, for some grave reason or necessity, she appears in public, or leaves off mourning, one day earlier than custom allows. It is a well-worn axiom, but not a perfect one, that the world is content with appearances. One should add, to make the axiom complete, that the world is never contented with, and often does not care about, and often is intolerant of, the substance. A famous ancient Roman tried harder to be good than to appear to be good, but the world demands of us to appear to be good, and not to be good.

56

Sincerity can be helpful when it is used with art, or when, because of its rarity, it is not trusted.

57

People are ashamed not of the injustices they do, but of those they receive. And so, in order that the unjust person should be ashamed, there is no other way than to give as good as one gets.

58

Those who are timid do not have less *amour propre* than those who are arrogant. Indeed, they have more – or more sensitive rather – *amour propre*. And so they are afraid, and they take care not to hurt others not because that matters more to them than to those who are insolent and bold, but to avoid being hurt themselves, considering the extreme pain they feel at every hurt they receive.

59

It is often said that the greater the decrease in real virtues in a country, the greater the increase in apparent virtues. It seems that literature is subject to the same fate, since in our time the more we lack the memory – I cannot say the use – of the virtues of style, the more the splendour of our publications grows. In other times, no classic book was printed as elegantly as newspapers are nowadays, and other political tittle-tattle, made to last a day. But the art of writing is no longer known, and its value is scarcely understood. And I believe that every decent man, on opening or reading a modern book, feels pity for those sheets of paper and that clear typeface, employed to represent words so horrid, and thoughts for the most part so idle.

60

La Bruyère was certainly right when he said that it is easier for a mediocre book to acquire fame by virtue of a reputation which its author has already obtained than it is for an author to acquire a reputation by means of an excellent book.* To this, one might add that the shortest way to acquire fame is to affirm, confidently and persistently, and in as many ways as possible, that one has already acquired it.

61

Once he has left his youth behind, a man has lost that power of communicating and, so to speak, inspiring others with his presence. And having lost that kind of influence which a young man has on those around him, and which links them to him, and always makes them feel some sort of inclination towards him, he realizes, not without unwonted pain, that in company he is separate from everyone else, and surrounded by sensitive creatures hardly less indifferent towards him than those deprived of sense.

62

Basic to one's readiness, on the right occasion, to sacrifice oneself for others is to have a high opinion of oneself.

63

The idea which the artist has of his art, or the scholar of his branch of knowledge, is usually great in inverse proportion to the idea which he has of his own worth in that art or branch of knowledge.

64

That artist or scholar or student in any discipline who is accustomed to comparing himself not with other people working in the same area but with the pursuit itself, the more outstanding he is, the lower the idea he will have of himself. This is because the greater understanding he has of the profundity of that art, the more inferior he will find himself by comparison. So it is that almost all great men are modest, because they continually compare themselves not with others, but with that idea of perfection which they have in their minds, infinitely clearer and greater than that which the common herd has, and so they see how far they are from achieving it. The common herd, on the contrary, and perhaps at times with truth, can easily believe that they have not only achieved, but surpassed that idea of perfection which they have in their minds.

65

No company is pleasing, in the long run, except that of people whose esteem we find more and more necessary or pleasing to us. Therefore women, who do not want their company to cease pleasing after a short while, ought to try to make themselves such that their esteem may be lastingly desired.

66

In the present century black people are believed to be by race and origin completely different from white people, and nevertheless completely equal to them in the matter of human rights. In the sixteenth century, when black people were believed to come from the same stock as white people, and to be of the same family, it was maintained, particularly by Spanish theologians, that in the matter of rights, they were by nature, and by divine will, very much inferior to us. And in both centuries black people were and are bought and sold, and made to work in chains under the lash. Such is ethics. We see how much beliefs in moral matters have to do with actions.

67

It is scarcely correct to say that boredom is a common complaint. It is common to be unemployed, or idle rather, but not to be bored. Boredom concerns only those in whom the spirit matters. The greater someone's spirit, the more frequent, painful and terrible is the boredom. Most people find that anything at all can keep them occupied, and any dull occupation gives them all the pleasure they need. And even when they are wholly unoccupied, they do not feel any great pain on that account. This is why men of feeling are so little understood concerning their boredom, and why they make the common herd marvel sometimes and sometimes laugh, when they speak of it and complain of it with such grave words as are used in connection with the greatest and most inevitable ills of life.

68

Boredom is in some ways the most sublime of human feelings. It is not that I think an examination of this feeling gives rise to those consequences that many philosophers have claimed to have inferred. Nevertheless, not being able to be satisfied with any earthly thing or, so to speak, with the whole earth; considering the immeasurable extent of space, the number and the wonderful size of the worlds, and finding that everything is small and petty in comparison with the capacity of one's own mind; picturing to oneself the infinite number of worlds, and the infinite universe, and feeling that the soul and our desire must be still greater than such a universe; always accusing things of insufficiency and nothingness; and suffering a huge lack and emptiness, and therefore boredom – all this seems to me the greatest sign of grandeur and nobility which there is in human nature. And so boredom is seldom seen in men of no account, and very seldom or never in other creatures.

69

From the famous letter of Cicero to Lucceius, persuading him to compose a history of the Catiline conspiracy, and from another letter not so widely known and no less curious, in which the Emperor Verus begs his tutor Fronto to write (as he did) of the Parthian War waged by Verus himself, letters very like those which today are written to journalists, except that the moderns ask for newspaper articles, while those, because they were ancients, asked for books – from these it is possible in some small way to deduce how truthful history is, even when it is written by contemporaries and men of great reputation in their time.

70

Many of those errors, thought of as childish ones, into which young men fall when they are unused to the world, as also do those who, young or old, are condemned by nature to be more than men and appear to be always boys, consist, if one considers carefully, solely in the fact that they think and behave as if men were less boyish than they are. Certainly what first and perhaps foremost strikes the minds of well-brought-up youngsters with wonder, at their entry into the world, is the frivolousness of the ordinary occupations, the pastimes, the conversations, the inclinations and the spirits of the people. With use they adapt to this frivolity little by little, but not without pain and difficulty, since it seems to them from the beginning that they have to become boys once more. And so it is. The young man who has a good character and is well bred, when he begins, as they say, to live, has to go backwards, and almost go into a second childhood, as it were. And he finds that he was very deceived in his belief that he had to become completely adult, and abandon every vestige of childhood. Because, on the contrary, most men, although they advance in years, for the most part always go on living in a childish way.

71

As a result of the opinion, mentioned above, which the young man has of men, believing them more adult than they are, he is dismayed by every fault he commits, and he thinks he has lost the respect of those who saw and were aware of his faults. After a short time he takes comfort again, not without surprise, seeing himself treated by them just as he was at first. People are not so ready to despise, since otherwise they would do nothing else, and they forget mistakes, because all the time they see and commit too many of them. And they are not so consistent that they do not easily admire today someone whom they may have derided yesterday. We know how often we ourselves blame someone or other, even with very stern words, or mock someone who is absent, without him going down in our estimation in any way at all, and neither is he treated, when he is present, any differently from before.

72

In the above-mentioned matter, the young man is deceived by his fear. Similarly, they are deceived by their hope who, realizing they have been lowered in someone's esteem or have lost it entirely, try to raise themselves by dint of performing services for him or affording him gratification. Respect is not gained by deference. Besides, respect is in one way no different from friendship in that it is like a flower that, once trampled on or withered, never blooms again. And so, from what we must regard as humiliating actions one gains nothing but greater scorn. It is true that anyone's contempt, even if it is unjust, is so painful to bear that few, when they suffer from it, are so strong as to do nothing. Rather, they devote themselves by various means, most of which are useless, to freeing themselves from it. And it is a very common habit of mediocre men to be haughty and disdainful with those whom they do not care about and with those who show concern for them, and then at the first sign or suspicion of indifference, to turn humble in order not to suffer it, and often to resort to humiliating deeds. For this reason also the way to behave when someone shows disdain is to repay him with signs of equal or greater disdain, because then there is every likelihood that you will see his pride turn into humility. And in any case he cannot fail to feel so offended, and at the same time feel such respect for you, that he will be punished enough.

73

Almost all women, and men very commonly too, and even the proudest, are won over and held on to by indifference and disdain – or rather, when necessary, by the pretence of not caring for them and having no respect for them. This is because that very pride which leads so many men to display hauteur with those who are humble, and with all those who give signs of honouring them, makes them caring and solicitous and needful of the respect and attention of those who do not care about them or who make a show of not being bothered about them. This is why it happens not seldom – in fact often, and not only in matters of love – that there grows to be a charming alternation between two people, with either one or the other, perpetually alternating, today cared about and not caring, tomorrow caring and not cared about. Indeed, it can be said that a similar alternation is played out in some way, more or less, in all of human society, and that every branch of life is full of people who when they are looked at do not look, who when they are greeted do not respond, who when they are followed flee, and who, when backs are turned on them and faces turn away, themselves turn and yield and run after others.

74

Towards great men, and particularly towards those who glow with an unusual virility, the world is like a woman. It does not merely admire them, it loves them, because of their vigour. Often, as with women, the love for such men is greater because of and in proportion to the disdain which they show and the ill treatment which they inflict, and the very fear which they inspire in men. Thus Napoleon was much loved in France, and became a cult, as it were, among the soldiers, whom he called cannon fodder and treated as such. Similarly, many captains, who thought of and used men in the same way, were much loved by their armies while they were alive, and histories of them make today's readers fall in love. Even a sort of brutality and eccentricity pleases not a little in such men, as it pleases women in their lovers. And so Achilles is perfectly lovable, while the goodness of Aeneas and Godfrey of Bouillon, as well as their wisdom and that of Ulysses, almost generate hatred.

75

There are several other ways in which woman is a symbol of the world at large. Weakness is a quality most men possess and, in relation to the few men who are strong of mind or of heart or of hand, it means that the majority are such as women usually are in relation to men. And so the human race is won over with more or less the same arts as women are. By ardour combined with gentleness, by putting up with repulses, by persevering steadily and without shame, one gets to the heart not only of women, but also of powerful people, of wealthy people, particularly of most men, of the nations and of the centuries. Just as with women it is necessary to knock

LEOPARDI

down one's rivals, and make a desert all round, so in the world it is necessary to floor one's equals and companions, and go forward over their bodies. And they and rivals in love are beaten by the same weapons, of which two principal ones are calumny and laughter. With women and with men, he who loves them with a love that is not feigned or lukewarm, and who puts their interests before his own, gets nowhere, or at least is very unfortunate. The world, like women, is for him who seduces it, enjoys it and walks all over it.

76

There is nothing rarer in the world than someone who is usually bearable.

77

Physical health is generally the last blessing to be thought of, and there are few important actions and affairs in life where health, if it is thought of at all, is not subordinated to all other considerations. The reason may be partly, but not entirely, that life is mainly the preserve of the healthy who always either despise what they possess or do not fear to lose it. As one example from a thousand, there are various reasons why a certain place is chosen on which to build a city, and reasons why the population of a city grows, but the healthiness of the site is seldom among these reasons. On the contrary, there is no site on earth so unhealthy and unpleasant that, if it offers opportunities, men do not willingly agree to live there. Often a most healthy, but uninhabited, place is in proximity to one that is not very healthy but is densely inhabited. Moreover, whole populations can continually be seen to forsake healthy cities and climates in order to come together under harsh skies, in places which not seldom are unhealthy, and sometimes almost pestilential, to which certain advantages invite them. London and Madrid are examples of cities with the worst possible conditions for health, whose populations, since they are capitals, are augmented daily by people leaving healthy dwellings in the provinces. Without going beyond our own regions, in Tuscany Leghorn, because of its trade, has from its first establishment constantly grown in population, and is still growing. Also, on the way to Leghorn, Pisa, a healthy place, and famed for its mild and temperate air, which was once full of people when it was a powerful and seafaring city, is now reduced to a desert almost, and goes on losing more people every day.

78

Two or more people in a public place or in any assembly who are noticeably laughing together, while others do not know what they are laughing about, cause such anxiety in all those present that every conversation becomes serious, many people fall silent, and some go away, while the boldest draw near to those who are laughing, endeavouring to be accepted so that they may laugh in company with them. It is just as if bursts of artillery fire were heard nearby, where there were people in the dark. Everyone would be thrown into confusion, not knowing who might be hit if the artillery were loaded with shot. Laughter gains esteem and respect even from strangers, attracts the attention of all those around, and gives one a sort of superiority among them. And if, as does happen, you find yourself at times somewhere where either you are ignored or treated arrogantly and discourteously, you need only choose from those present one who looks as though he will do, and laugh with him frankly and openly and perseveringly, showing as well as you can that the laughter comes from your heart. If some there are laughing at you, you must laugh more clearly and more constantly than they do. You will be very unfortunate if the proudest and most impudent in the company, and those who most turned their faces away from you, when they notice your laughter do not, after only a brief resistance, either turn to flight or come of their own accord to beg for peace, seeking out your conversation, and perhaps offering themselves as friends. The power of laughter is great among men and causes great terror. No one finds his own mind completely armed against it. He who has the courage to laugh is master of the world, much like him who is prepared to die.

79

A young man never learns the art of living – never has, one might say, success in society, and never experiences any pleasure in it – while the vehemence of his desires lasts. The more he cools down, the more capable he is of dealing with other people and himself. Nature, benign as ever, has ordained that the more man learns to live, the more the reasons for living desert him; that he must not know the means of achieving his ends until he ceases to regard them as heavenly felicities, when obtaining them does not bring him more than a mediocre joy; and that he must not be pleased until he has become incapable of lively pleasure. Many find themselves in this state when they are very young, and often they do well, because their desires are slight, and in their minds adulthood has, through a convergence of experience and intellect, come before its time. Others never reach this state in all their lives. They are those few whose strength of feeling is so great to begin with that it never fails throughout the years. These people more than all others would enjoy life, if Nature had meant life to be enjoyed. But they are very unhappy, and until death they remain children in the ways of the world, which they are unable to learn.

80

When I see again after a few years someone whom I knew when he was young, he at first always looks to me like one who has suffered some great misfortune. A joyful and confident appearance belongs only to youth, and the sense of what one is losing, and of the physical disorders which from day to day grow worse, produces in even the most frivolous or those who are happy by nature, and likewise even in the happiest, a habitual expression of the face and a behaviour which is called grave, and which, in contrast to that of young people and children, is truly wretched.

81

It is in conversation as it is with writers. At the beginning many writers, once we find that they have new ideas and their own opinions, please greatly, but then, as we go on reading, they become boring, because parts of their writing are imitations of other parts. So it is in conversation, for new people are often prized and welcome on account of their ways and their words, and as we get used to them, they become boring and fall in our esteem, because people inevitably, some more and some less, when they do not imitate others, imitate themselves. And so those who travel, especially if they are men of some intelligence who practise the art of conversation, readily leave behind them, in the places through which they pass, an opinion of themselves which is far above the truth, given the opportunity they have of hiding what is the usual defect of the human spirit, I mean its poverty. This is because everything they reveal on one or only a few occasions, when they speak mainly of those matters which most concern them, towards which they are led, even without their employing any artifice, by the courtesy and curiosity of others, is believed to be not their entire inward riches, but the least part of it, and, so to speak, loose change to spend as they wish, and certainly not, as perhaps it most often is, either all they possess or the greater part of their money. And this belief remains strong, for lack of new occasions that might destroy it. For the same reasons travellers for their part also are likely to make mistakes, judging too highly of people of some ability whom they come across in their travels.

82

No one becomes a man before he has had considerable experience of himself – which, revealing himself to himself, and determining his own opinion of himself, in some ways determines his fortune and his state in life. For this great experience, before which no one in the world is much more than a child, life in ancient times provided infinite available material, but today private life is so poor in incident, and of such a nature for everyone, that, for lack of opportunity, many men die before the experience I speak of, and so are like babies, little more than if they had not been born. To others self-knowledge and self-possession usually come either from needs and misfortunes or from some grand – by which I mean strong – passion. This is most often the passion of love, when love is a grand passion (something which is not experienced by all who love). However, if it does occur, either at the start of life, as it does for some, or later and after other loves of less importance, as seems to happen more often, then certainly when a man issues from a grand and passionate love, he is scarcely conscious of his fellows among whom he has to move with his intense desires and with his grave needs never perhaps experienced before. He knows *ab esperto** the nature of the passions (since if one of them is blazing, it inflames all the others), he knows his own nature and temperament, he has got the measure of his own abilities and strengths, and by now he can judge himself and what he must hope for or despair of from himself – and, in so far as the future can be foretold, what place he is destined to have in the world. In short, in his eyes life has taken on a different appearance, being changed for him from a thing heard of to a thing seen, from something imagined to something real, and he feels he is in the middle of it, perhaps not happier but, so to speak, more powerful than before, that is more apt to make good use of himself and of others.

83

If those few men of true worth who pursue glory knew individually all those who compose that public whose esteem they try to gain with so many and such extreme sufferings, it is possible that their purpose would be considerably weakened, and they might perhaps abandon it. However, we cannot escape the power which the sheer number of people has over our imagination, and it is noticeable time and time again that we appreciate, indeed respect, I will not say a multitude, but ten people gathered in one room, each one of whom by himself we regard as of no account.

84

Jesus Christ was the first to point out to us distinctly that praiser and teacher of all the feigned virtues; that detractor and persecutor of all the true ones; that enemy of all the greatness which is intrinsic to and really characteristic of mankind; that derider of all elevated feeling, unless he believes it to be false, and of all tender affection, if he believes it to be heartfelt; that slave of the strong, tyrant of the weak, hater of the unhappy; to whom Jesus Christ gave the name of "the world", with a meaning which it still has in all civilized languages up to the present day. I do not believe that before that time this general idea, which contains such truth, and which has been and always will be of such utility, had occurred to anyone else, nor do I recall its being found, I mean in one word and in such a precise form, in any pagan philosopher. Perhaps this is because before that time meanness and fraud had not grown so mature, and civilization had not got to the stage where it had become confused with corruption.

In short, such as I have described above, and such as was indicated by Jesus Christ, is the man whom they call civilized, that man whom reason and intellect do not reveal, whom books and educators do not announce, whom nature constantly says is mythical and whom only experience of life causes to be known and believed to be true. And it is noteworthy that the idea which I have described, although it is a general one, is found to fit innumerable individuals exactly.

85

We never find in pagan writers that the generality of civilized people, whom we call society or the world, is considered or shown as the determined enemy of virtue, or as the certain corruptor of every good character, and of every developing mind. The world as the enemy of the good is a concept that is as frequent in the gospels and in modern writers, even secular ones, as it is more or less unknown to the ancients. And this will not surprise anyone who considers one very simple and obvious fact, which can serve as an instance for anyone who wishes to compare the ancients and moderns in moral matters. Where modern educators fear the public, the ancients sought it, and where the moderns use domestic obscurity, segregation and seclusion as a protection for young people against the plague of worldly habits, the ancients took their young people, by force even, out of their solitude, and exposed their education and their life to the eyes of the world, and the world to their eyes, because they considered the example likelier to teach than to corrupt.

86

The most certain way to conceal the limits of one's own knowledge is not to go beyond them.

87

He who travels much has this advantage over others: that the things he remembers soon become remote, so that in a short time they acquire that vague and poetical quality which is only given to other things by time. He who has not travelled at all has this disadvantage: that all his memories are of things present somewhere, since the places with which all his memories are concerned are present.

88

It happens not seldom that people who are vain and full of their own conceit, instead of being egoistic and hard, as would seem likely, are pleasant, kind, good companions, and also good friends and very helpful. Since they think that everyone admires them, it is only reasonable that they should love those whom they believe to be their admirers, and help them whenever they can, simply because they believe that this is right and proper, considering the superiority with which fate has favoured them. They converse willingly, because they believe the world resounds with their name, and they are tender in their ways, secretly praising themselves for their affability, and for knowing how to adapt their greatness to this mingling with little people. And I have noticed that, as their opinion of themselves grows, so they grow too in benignity. Finally, the certainty which they have of their own importance, and of the consensus of the human race in admitting it, takes away all roughness from their manners, because no one who is content with himself and other men has coarse habits, and generates in them such tranquillity that sometimes they take on the appearance of modest people.

89

He who has little communication with people is seldom a misanthrope. True misanthropes are not found in solitude, but in the world. This is because it is practical experience of life, and certainly not philosophy, that makes people hate their fellows. And if someone who is a misanthrope withdraws from society, in his seclusion he loses his misanthropy.

90

I once knew a little boy who, when he was crossed in anything by his mother, used to say, "Oh, I see, I see! Mummy's being naughty." The majority of people use the same logic when they talk of their nearest and dearest, although they do not express themselves quite so plainly.

91

Whoever introduces you to someone, if he wishes to commend you effectively, should leave aside your more real and distinctive qualities, and mention the more external ones and those that you owe more to fortune. If you are great and powerful in the world, he should say great and powerful; if rich, he should say rich; if nothing but noble, he should say noble. He should not say magnanimous, or virtuous, or polite, or fond, or anything similar (unless as a mere addition), even if you do possess these qualities, and to a high degree. And if you are lettered, and in some places celebrated for being so, he should not say learned, or profound, or very talented, or outstanding. Rather he should say celebrated. As I have said elsewhere, it is fortune that is favoured in the world, and not worth.

92

Jean-Jacques Rousseau says that true courtesy consists of habitually showing oneself to be kind. This sort of courtesy may perhaps preserve you from hatred, but it will not gain you love, except from those few to whom other people's kindness acts as a stimulus to reciprocate. Whoever wishes, as far as one can with manners, to make people his friends, or his lovers even, should show that he esteems them. Just as contempt hurts and displeases more than hatred, so esteem is sweeter than kindness, and generally men take more care, or certainly have more desire, to be esteemed than loved. Demonstrations of esteem, true or false (since either way they are believed by those who are the objects of them), almost always win gratitude. And many who would not lift a finger to help someone who truly loves them are filled with immediate affection for anyone who appears to esteem them. Such demonstrations are very effective even in reconciling those we have offended, because it seems that it is not in our human nature to hate someone who expresses esteem for us. At the same time, it is not merely a possibility, but something often observed, that people hate and avoid those who love them, and even those who benefit them. For if the art of winning people over by conversation consists of ensuring that others depart from us happier with themselves than they were before, it is obvious that signs of esteem will be more valid to win men over than signs of kindness. And the less esteem is due, the more efficacious it is to show it. Those who have this habitual courtesy are more or less courted wherever they go, because people gather, like flies round a honey pot, round that sweet belief that they are esteemed. And for the most part those who praise are themselves highly praised, because from the praises which they, in conversation, offer to everyone else, there grows a great harmony of praise which everyone gives to them, partly out of gratitude, and partly because it is in our interest that those who esteem us should be praised and esteemed. In this way people, without realizing it, and individually possibly against their will, through their agreement in celebrating such people, elevate them socially far above themselves, to whom such people continually show signs of holding themselves inferior.

93

Many of those, indeed almost all, who are believed by themselves and by their acquaintances to be well reputed in society, really have only the esteem of one particular company, or of one class, or of one kind of person, to whom they belong and among whom they live. The man of letters, who believes himself to be famous and respected in the world, finds himself either left on one side or scorned every time he comes across the company of frivolous people, who make up three quarters of the world. The young gallant, made much of by women and by his peers, is neglected and confused in the society of businessmen. The courtier, whom his companions and dependants overwhelm with ceremony, is held up to ridicule and forsaken by fair-weather friends. I conclude, to make it plain, that a man cannot hope for, and consequently should not wish to win, the esteem, as they say, of society, but of a small number of people. As for the others, he should be content to be completely ignored sometimes, and sometimes more or less despised, because this is a fate that cannot be escaped.

94

He who has never gone beyond his own tiny locality, where petty ambitions and vulgar avarice reign, together with an intense hatred felt by everyone for everyone else, regards as mere myth sincere and stable social virtues, just as he does great vices. And as for friendship, he believes it to be something found in poems and stories, not in life. And he is wrong. No Pylades or Pirithous* certainly, but good, affable friends really are found in the world, and they are not rare. The services which may be expected or requested from such friends, I mean such friends as the world really gives, are either of words, which often turn out to be very useful, or even at times of deeds, but all too seldom of goods, which the wise and prudent man should never request. It is easier to find someone who puts his life in danger for a stranger than one who, I shall not say spends, but risks one *scudo* for a friend.

95

And men do have some excuse for this. It is a rare person who genuinely has more than he needs, since our needs depend almost entirely on habituation, and since our expenditure is usually proportionate to our wealth, if not greater. And those few who accumulate without spending, have a need to accumulate, either for projects of theirs or for possible necessities which may lie in the future. Nor is it significant if one need or another is imaginary, because there are all too few things in life which do not exist wholly or mainly in the imagination.

96

The honest man, in the course of years, easily becomes insensitive to praise and honour, but never, I believe, to blame or contempt. Indeed, the praise and esteem of many outstanding people may not compensate for the pain he feels at one hurtful word or one sign of indifference from some man of no account. Perhaps the opposite is the case with scoundrels, for, being used to blame and unused to real praise, they may be insensitive to the former, but not to the latter, if ever they chance to have some experience of it.

97

It may seem a paradox, but with experience of life one realizes its truth, that those people whom the French call originals are not only not rare, but are so common that I was about to say that it is rarer to find in society a man who truly is not what is called an original. I am not speaking of minor differences from man to man; I am speaking of qualities and ways of his own that a man has, and that to others prove to be strange, bizarre, absurd. I am also saying that seldom will you have to do for a long time even with someone who is very civilized, without discovering in him and his ways more than one strangeness or absurdity or bizarrerie, such as to make you marvel.

You will come to this discovery sooner with others than with the French, sooner perhaps with mature men or old people than with youngsters, who often have the ambition of conforming to others, and who moreover, if they are well brought up, apply more strength to themselves. But sooner or later you will discover this in the end in the majority of those with whom you have dealings. In short, nature's variety is so great that it is impossible for civilization, for all its tendency to make people uniform, to conquer nature.

98

A similar observation to that above is the following. Anyone who has or has had anything to do with men, if he thinks it over a little, will remember having been not many times but very many times a spectator, and perhaps taken part, in scenes which are, as they say, real, but which differ in no way from those which, if seen in the theatre, or read in comedies or novels, are believed to be fictionalized beyond what is natural, for the sake of art. All this means simply that wickedness, foolishness, vices of every kind and the ridiculous qualities and actions of men, are much more usual than we think, and that perhaps we shall not be believable if we go beyond those limits which mark off what is regarded as normal from what is supposed to be exaggerated.

99

People are not ridiculous except when they wish to seem or be what they are not. The poor, the ignorant, the rustic, the sick, the old are never ridiculous while they are content to appear such, and while they keep within the limits imposed by their condition. But they certainly are ridiculous when the old man wants to seem young, the sick man healthy, the poor man rich, and the ignorant man wants to act like an educated man, the rustic like a city dweller. Even physical defects, however serious they may be, would provoke nothing more than a passing smile if the sufferer did not try to hide them, that is, want to seem not to have them, to be different from what he is. If we consider carefully, we shall see that our defects or disadvantages are not in themselves ridiculous. What is ridiculous is the effort we make to hide them, and our wanting to act as though we did not have them.

Those who, in order to make themselves more lovable, affect a moral character different from their own, make a great mistake. The very effort, which after a short time it is impossible to keep up without its becoming obvious, and the opposition between the feigned character and the real one, which from the start keeps coming through, render him more unlovable and more displeasing than he would be if he showed himself as he was frankly and constantly. Even the most wretched character has something in it which is not unpleasant and which, because it is real, if it were brought out at the right moment, would please much more than the finest feigned quality.

Generally, wanting to be what we are not spoils everything in the world. Very many people are unbearable for no other reason, although they would be very likeable if only they would be content to be themselves. And not only individuals, but gatherings of people, indeed whole populations. And I know several cultured and flourishing provincial cities which would be very pleasant to live in, if it were not for their nauseating imitation of the capitals, their wanting to be, as far as is in them, capital rather than provincial cities.

100

Thinking of the defects or disadvantages which people may have, I do not deny that the world is seldom like those judges who are forbidden by law to condemn a criminal, however convinced they are of his guilt, if the man himself does not explicitly confess to the crime. Nevertheless, although hiding with manifest zeal one's own defects is a ridiculous thing, I would not recommend that they should confess of their own free will, and certainly not give people to understand that their defects make them inferior to others. That would only be to condemn oneself by that final judgement which the world, as long as one holds one's head up, never gets round to pronouncing. In this kind of struggle of each against all, and of all against each, in which, if we want to call things by their proper names, social life consists, with everyone endeavouring to knock his companion down in order to put his foot on him, he makes a great mistake who prostrates himself, or even bows, or even inclines his head willingly. There is no doubt (except when these things are done in pretence, as a stratagem) that he will be walked all over and trampled on by his neighbours, without any courtesy or pity in the world. This is a mistake which young people almost always make, and especially when they are of a polite disposition. Time and again they admit, without necessity or relevance, their disadvantages and misfortunes. They are moved partly by the frankness that is natural at their age, which makes them hate dissimulation and enjoy affirming the truth, even against themselves, and partly, since they are themselves generous, by the hope of obtaining by this means pardon and favour from the world for their misfortunes. And in that golden age of their life, they are so far ignorant of the truth of human affairs that they make a display of unhappiness, thinking that this makes them lovable, and wins people over to them. Nor, to be honest, are they unreasonable in thinking this. Only long and constant personal experience can persuade people who are themselves kind that the world will pardon anything more readily than misfortune, that it is not unhappiness, but fortune that wins favour, and that therefore it is not the former, but the latter, of which one should always, as far as possible, even in despite of the truth, make display. They need to know that the confession of one's ills does not occasion pity but pleasure, does not sadden but delights, not only enemies but everyone who hears it, because it is, as it were, a sign of one's own inferiority and other people's superiority, and that, since man can trust nothing on earth but his strength, he should never willingly yield anything or retreat one step, much less surrender at his enemy's discretion, but defend himself and resist to the very end, and fight obstinately to retain or acquire, if he can, even despite fortune, what he will never gain by his supplications to the generosity or humanity of his neighbours. I myself believe that no one ought even to allow anyone in his presence to call him unhappy or unfortunate. These words in almost all languages were, and are, synonyms for wicked, perhaps from ancient superstition, as if unhappiness were the penalty for wickedness. Certainly in all languages they are and will continue to be offensive, because he who uses them, whatever his intention, feels that by them he elevates himself and lowers his companion, and the same is felt by him who hears them.

101

By confessing his own infirmities, however obvious they may be, a man causes manifold harm to the esteem, and hence to the affection, which his nearest and dearest have for him. So it is necessary that everyone should stand up for himself strongly, whatever his state, and that despite any of his misfortunes, by showing he has a firm and secure respect for himself, he should give an example for others to respect him, and, as it were, constrain them by his own authority. If a man's estimation does not come from himself, it is hard to see how it will come from anywhere else, and if it does not have a solid foundation in him, it will hardly stand firm. Human society is like fluids. Every particle of a fluid, or tiny drop, pressing strongly on its neighbours above and below and on all sides, and pressing through them on the most distant drops, and being pressed in its turn in the same way, if at some place the resistance and the mutual pushing grow less, not an instant passes before the whole mass of the fluid rushes together towards that place, and the space is occupied by new drops.

102

The years of youth are, in everyone's memory, the legendary times of his life. Similarly, in the memory of a nation, the legendary times are those of the nation's youth.

103

Praise given to us has the power of making us esteem subjects and faculties we have formerly scorned every time that we happen to be praised for anything of such a kind.

104

The sort of education given, especially in Italy, to those who are educated (who, to tell the truth, are not many) is a formal betrayal ordained by weakness against strength, by old age against youth. Old people come and say to young people, "Avoid the pleasures natural to your time of life, since they are all dangerous and contrary to good behaviour, and because we, who have enjoyed them as much as we were able, and who would do the same again if we could, are no longer capable of them, because of our years. Do not bother about living today, but be obedient, suffer and strive as hard as you know how in order to live when it will be too late. Wisdom and decorum require that the young abstain as far as possible from making use of their youth, except to surpass others in hard work. Leave the care of your destiny and everything important to us, who will direct everything to our advantage. At your age every one of us did quite the opposite of what we are recommending, and we would do the same again if we were young once more. But you must pay attention to our words, and not to what we did in the past, or to our intentions. Believe us, who are wise and experienced in human affairs: if you act as we say, you will be happy." I do not know what deceit and fraud are, if they do not consist of promising happiness to the inexperienced upon such conditions.

The interests of general tranquillity, domestic and public, are opposed to the pleasures and enterprises of young people. And so even a good education, or what is called such, consists in great part of deceiving pupils into subordinating their own advantage to that of others. But even without this, old people naturally tend to destroy the young, as far as they can, and to obliterate them from human life, since they abhor the sight of them. In all times old age has conspired against youth, because in all times it has been natural for men basely to condemn and persecute in others those blessings that they would rather keep for themselves. Nevertheless, it is still noteworthy that, among educators – who, if they are people of the world, profess to want their neighbours' good – there are so many who try to deprive their pupils of the greatest blessing in life, which is youth. It is even more noteworthy that fathers and mothers, not to mention other tutors, never feel pangs of conscience for giving their children an education based on such a malign principle. This would be even more surprising if for a long time, for other reasons, trying to abolish youth had not been regarded as a meritorious effort.

The result of such a pernicious culture, intent on benefiting the cultivator with the ruin of the plant, is either that the pupils, having lived like old people in the first bloom of their lives, make themselves ridiculous and unhappy when they are old, by trying to live like young people, or rather, as happens more often, Nature wins, and young people, living as young people despite their education, rebel against the educators, who, if they had encouraged the use and enjoyment of youthful faculties, would have been able to regulate them through the confidence their pupils would have had in their teachers, which they would never have lost.

105

Shrewdness, which belongs to the intellect, is employed most often to make up for a scarcity of intellect, and to overcome a greater abundance of intellect in others.

106

The world laughs at those things that otherwise it would have to admire, and it reprehends, like the fox in Aesop,* what it envies. A great love affair, with great consolations after great torments, is universally envied, and so reprehended the more severely. A habit of being generous, or a heroic action, ought to be admired, but people, if they admired, especially among equals, would think themselves humiliated. And so, instead of admiring, they laugh. This goes so far that in social life noble actions need to be dissimulated more carefully than base actions. Everyone is base, and so that is at least pardoned. But nobility goes against the custom and seems to indicate presumption, or beg praise, which the public, and acquaintances particularly, do not like to give with sincerity.

107

Most stupid things are said in company through a desire to talk. But the young man who has some self-respect when he first enters into society easily errs in another way. In speaking he expects that extraordinary things of some beauty and importance will occur to him to say. With such expectations, what happens is that he never speaks. The most sensible conversation in the world, and the most spirited, is one composed for the most part of frivolous or trite discourse, which anyhow serves to pass the time in speaking. And everyone has to decide to say things that are for the most part commonplace, in order just sometimes to say things that are not commonplace.

108

Men make great efforts, while they are immature, to seem like grown men, and once they are grown-up, to seem immature. Oliver Goldsmith, the author of the novel *The Vicar of Wakefield*, once he had reached the age of forty took the title of doctor from his address, because at that age such a demonstration of gravity had become hateful to him, although it had been dear to him in his early years.*

109

Men are almost always as wicked as they need to be. When they act honestly, one may be sure that wickedness is not necessary to them. I have seen people of very good habits, completely innocent people, commit the most atrocious actions, in order to avoid some grave harm which was not avoidable in any other way.

110

It is curious that almost all men of worth have simple manners, and that simple manners are almost always taken as a sign of little worth.

111

A habit of silence during conversation pleases and is praised when it is known that the person who is silent has, when necessary, both the boldness and the aptitude for speech.

Notes

p. 9, *three great nations*: England, France and Germany.

p. 36, *such as... in Greek*: In English the word "simple" is analogous in its use to the Italian and Greek words Leopardi mentions.

p. 39, *Guicciardini... will of others*: The quote is from Chapter XVII of *Storia d'Italia* (1537–40) by Francesco Guicciardini (1483–1540).

p. 42, *Buffon... present danger*: This is from 'De la vieillesse et de la mort' ('Of Old Age and Death'), *Histoire naturelle*, vol. II (1749), by Georges-Louis Leclerc, Comte de Buffon (1707–88).

p. 44, *La Bruyère... excellent book*: This is from 'Des ouvrages de l'esprit' ('Of the Works of the mind'), 4, *Caractères* (1688) by Jean de La Bruyère (1645–96).

p. 57, *ab esperto*: The same Latin expression (meaning "from experience") is used by Petrarch in his *Canzoniere*, CCCLV, 4. Leopardi is subtly bringing the authority of this great poet of love to bear on what he says.

p. 63, *Pylades or Pirithous*: In Greek mythology, they were famous for their friendship to Orestes and Theseus respectively.

p. 72, *like the fox in Aesop*: Having lost his own tail in a trap, the fox suggests that other foxes cut off their tails to follow the new fashion.

p. 73, *Oliver Goldsmith... early years*: This anecdote about Oliver Goldsmith (1728–74) could be found in various contemporary sources.

Extra Material

on

Giacomo Leopardi's

Thoughts

Leopardi's Life

Giacomo Leopardi was born on 29th June 1798 into what he *Birth*
was to describe as "a noble family in an ignoble city of Italy".
The city was Recanati, near to Ancona in the region known
now as Le Marche, and his parents were Count Monaldo
Leopardi and the Marchesa Adelaide Antici, both natives
of that city. Giacomo's noble origins were not in doubt: his
father's family had records which went back to 1200, and
his mother's family was also very ancient. Opinions of the
city, however, varied: Monaldo saw it, and not the land of
Italy, as his homeland and loved it; on the other hand a man
of letters who became Giacomo's friend, Pietro Giordani,
described it as "a little village which the Pope calls a city; it
is only four miles from Loreto, that huge market of ignoble
superstitions... All the ills of Italy are there, without any
consolation". It is not surprising that Giacomo's parents,
as aristocrats living in one of the Papal States, had no truck
with the ideal of Italian unification and self-rule which was
current during the nineteenth century – an ideal only realized
over twenty years after Giacomo's death. And his parents had
nothing but hatred for the subversive ideas and martial law
imported into their city by the French revolutionary armies
when Giacomo was only one year old.

Monaldo, whose intellect tends to be disparaged in com- *Father*
parison with his eldest son's, was a man with intellectual
interests and the author of many books, including an autobiography. The account in it of the French occupation of
Recanati, the civil disturbances which resulted, the danger to the
Leopardi family, and the sentence of death which was passed on
Monaldo himself (which was very nearly carried out) makes for
lively reading. Monaldo comes across as a rather self-satisfied

and pompous man, a conservative in politics and religion who, as he tells us, dressed always in black and "wore a sword every day, like the ancient knights... probably the last sword-bearer of Italy". He did his best to promote the education of his children and, although his eldest son at an early age educated himself beyond his father's understanding, their estrangement was a purely intellectual and religious one, which never prevented their being very fond of each other. In his early years – for he came into his inheritance when he was only eighteen – Monaldo had, as a result of the depredations of the French and of his own ineptitude and ill-advised specu-lation, found the family fortunes so far reduced that he was obliged to transfer all financial affairs into his wife's capable hands, where they remained. Despite his financial straits, Monaldo did manage to acquire a library of thousands of books which in 1812 he opened to the public (in theory at least, since it seems that no one from outside the family ever entered it). A Latin inscription above the door stated that it was for the use of his children, friends, and fellow citizens. The library's rather miscellaneous, and even random, composition, with a high proportion of theological volumes, is accounted for by the fact that much of it had been acquired in bulk, sometimes simply by weight, in the sales from religious foundations closed down during the French occupation of the city. The person who benefited most from this library was of course Giacomo.

Mother   Giacomo's mother Adelaide was clearly the dominant partner in the marriage. From all accounts, she had two aims in life, which she pursued without deviation. One was the preservation, by means of strict economy, of the way of life which she regarded as suitable for a noble family: appearances were always kept up despite difficult circumstances. Her other aim was the education of her children according to her own narrow interpretation of Christianity. Giacomo has left a chilling description of her:

> I have known intimately a mother who was not at all superstitious, but very staunch and precise in her Christian faith, and in the exercise of her religion. Not only was she not sorry for those parents who lost their children in infancy, but she envied them deeply and sincerely, since those children had flown safely to paradise, and had freed their parents from the bother of supporting them. Finding

herself several times in danger of losing her children at the same age, she did not pray God to make them die, because religion would not permit that, but she was truly delighted; and seeing her husband weeping or in distress, she withdrew into herself, obviously really annoyed. She was very precise in the care which she took of those poor patients, but in her heart of hearts she hoped it would be in vain, and went so far as to confess that the only dread she had when she questioned or consulted the doctors, was in hearing opinions or reports of an improvement. Seeing in the patients some signs of approaching death, she felt a deep joy (which she endeavoured to conceal only from those who condemned it), and the day of their death, if it came, was for her a happy and pleasant day, and she could not understand how her husband was so unwise as to be sad about it. She considered beauty a real misfortune, and seeing her children ugly or deformed, she thanked God for it, not out of heroism, but with all her heart. She did not try in any way to help them to hide their defects; rather did she require that, in view of those defects, they should renounce life completely in their first youth. If they resisted, if they tried to do the opposite, if they succeeded in that in the slightest, she was annoyed, and with her comments and opinions depreciated their successes as much as possible (of the ugly as of the handsome ones, for she had many children), and did not let an occasion slip, indeed looked diligently for the chance, to reproach them and make them well aware of their defects, and the consequences to be expected from them, and to persuade them of their inevitable unhappiness, with a pitiless and fierce veracity. She found real consolation in the ill success of her children in these and similar matters; and she dwelt by preference with them on what she had heard to their disadvantage. All this was to free them from the danger to their souls. She behaved in the same way in everything that concerned the education of the children, bringing them into the world, finding them a position in it, all the ways to worldly happiness. She felt infinite compassion for sinners, but very little for physical or worldly misfortunes, except when her own nature at times got the better of her. The illnesses, the most pitiful deaths of young people cut off in the flower of life, with all their great hopes, with the greatest loss to their family and to the public, etc., did not touch her in any way. For she said that it was not the year of death that mattered, but the manner, and therefore she used always to enquire diligently whether they had died well according to religion, or, when they were ill, if they were showing resignation etc. And she spoke of these calamities with a marmoreal coldness. This woman had been endowed by nature with a very sensitive disposition, and had been reduced to this state by religion alone.

This passage, which tallies with what Giacomo's sister Paolina had to say about her mother in rather more gentle terms, suggests from whom Giacomo inherited his mental ruthlessness in the pursuit of the truth as he saw it; it makes us wonder too if the emphasis he so often lays on the value of life on earth comes partly as a reaction to his mother's complete denial of it. Unlike most of those in her circle, Adelaide Leopardi seems to have seldom put pen to paper, and her outlook has to be gathered from other people's remarks and actions, but we always sense her presence in the background of Giacomo's life, particularly on those occasions when he had to ask his father for money and his father had to approach his wife for it.

Siblings   The other children in the family who mattered most to Giacomo were his brother Carlo, one year younger, with whom he was always on good terms, and his beloved sister Paolina, two years younger, who in her letters shows something of the keen intelligence of Giacomo. As a woman, it was even harder for her than for Giacomo to escape from the close confines of family life, and she managed to travel beyond Recanati only at the very end of her life.

Studies   The children's education was entrusted to a Jesuit father who was kept in the house for that purpose, and who had earlier been Monaldo's tutor. The basis of their education was ancient languages and philology. When Giacomo was fourteen, however, his tutor admitted that there was nothing more he could teach the boy, and this instruction was discontinued. Giacomo had already been studying a great deal by himself, and this he continued to do, passing most of his time in his father's great library in Palazzo Leopardi. Quite independently, he taught himself Greek and acquired considerable mastery in that language: indeed, he said that it was reading the poets of ancient Greece which first led him to think he was himself a poet.

Carlo, who slept in the same room as Giacomo, remembered seeing his brother burning the midnight oil night after night and only going to bed when the light gave out. Giacomo himself records how he gave himself up to years of "mad and desperate study". There is an indication of the unremitting effort he put into his studies in his description of how he learnt English: when he had written a page of whatever he was composing at the time, he memorized English vocabulary while he waited for the ink to dry. Not surprisingly, this way of life had an effect on his health, and he grew up to suffer from a number of serious ailments, of which the most obvious to those around him was a severe malformation of his back. This became apparent after the age of twelve, but strangely – although more than one relative pointed out to Monaldo the ill effects of Giacomo's way of life on his health, and Monaldo's brother-in-law offered to have him living with his family in Rome for a while to give him or force him to take some respite – Monaldo did nothing to help, and in fact admitted frankly that he could not have borne his son's absence. And he was not to let even his adult son go without a struggle.

Although it is important to emphasize Giacomo's life of furious study, there is ample evidence too of his boisterousness and love of horseplay when a child. In later life this became material, as so often with him, from which to draw a general conclusion:

> When I was a boy, I used to say sometimes to one of my brothers: "You shall be my horse." And having tied a small cord to him, I used to lead him as though by a bridle and hit him with a whip. And they were pleased to let me do it, and this did not make them any the less my brothers. I often remember this when I see a man (often of no worth) respectfully waited upon by this person or that in a hundred trifles, which he could do for himself, or just as well for those who are serving him, and perhaps have a greater need of it than he, who at times is probably healthier and stronger than those he has around him. And I say to myself, "My brothers were not horses, but human beings like myself, and these servants are human beings like their master..."

Without wishing to draw any generalization from the fact, it is pleasant also to record that in this usually solemn household the imposing full suit of armour standing at the entrance to the library, complete with lance and heraldically decorated shield, was known familiarly to the children as "Maurizio".

From the age of ten Giacomo was required to make presentations to his family to show how his studies were progressing, and from then until the end of his life his literary production was enormous. It included historical, philosophical and philological works and translations from Greek and Latin. One composition, which he published in a periodical as the translation of an ancient Greek hymn to Neptune, was so persuasive that there were people who believed that a Greek original did exist.

When he was nineteen something occurred which is not unusual in a boy of his age, but was unusual in setting a pattern which repeated itself more than once later in his life. He fell deeply and hopelessly in love and enjoyed the experience, even the pain of it, without hoping for any return of love. A twenty-seven-year-old cousin of his father's, Geltrude Cassi Lazzari, stayed with her husband overnight at Palazzo Leopardi as a stopover on a journey. The effect she had on Giacomo, quite unconsciously one presumes, is recorded in his poem 'First Love' and also in a long prose account.

Although Monaldo liked to attribute his son's alienation from the family ways and beliefs to the influence of friends from other parts of Italy with whom Giacomo corresponded, and who tended to have disturbing political and religious views, the causes went much deeper:

> In its poetic career my spirit has gone through the same phases as the human spirit in general. From the beginning my forte was fancy, and my verses were full of images, and I always tried to make my reading of poetry beneficial to the imagination. I was also indeed very sensitive to the affections, but I did not know how to express them in poetry. I had not yet meditated on things, and I had only a glimmer of philosophy – and this in broad terms, and with that usual illusion which we create for ourselves that in the world and in life an exception must always be made in our favour. I have always been unfortunate, but my misfortunes were at that time full of life, and I gave myself up to despair because it seemed to me (not indeed to my reason, but to a very firm fancy of mine) that my

misfortunes prevented me from having that happiness which I believed others enjoyed. In brief my state was exactly like that of the ancients... The whole change in me, and the passage from the ancient state to the modern, happened one might say within a year, that is 1819, when, deprived of the use of my eyes, and of the continual distraction of reading, I began to feel my unhappiness in a much more gloomy way – I began to abandon hope, to reflect deeply on things (under the influence of these thoughts I wrote in one year almost double what I had written in a year and a half, and on subjects which concern above all our nature, unlike my past thoughts, almost all of literature), to become a professed philosopher (from being a poet), to feel the assured unhappiness of the world, instead of just being acquainted with it, and this also through a state of physical weakness, which made me less like the ancients and more like the moderns.

That was the year when Giacomo made his first attempt to escape from Recanati, where he felt he was in an intellectual and psychological prison. He wrote to a family friend in Macerata, Count Xaverio Broglio d'Aiano, asking him in his father's name for a passport, such as was then essential for travelling between the different states of Italy. He himself had to write the description which the passport required:

Age 21 years. Low in stature. Hair black. Eyebrows black. Eyes light blue. Nose ordinary. Mouth regular. Chin likewise. Complexion pale.

This description omits what must have been his most obvious physical characteristic – the hump on his back – why, we can only speculate. His intention was to leave Recanati in secret and go to Milan, where he had friends who would, he hoped, provide him with employment and therefore the means to live. From Macerata Monaldo got some inkling of the plan, and the passport was sent, but to him and not to his son, and Giacomo backed down and the attempted flight came to nothing but great upset on all sides.

Carlo has testified to the dreadful psychological state that Giacomo was in during this period, when at times the only alternative to flight that he could see was suicide. His hatred of

Recanati, so often and so fervently expressed, cannot obscure, however, the fact that the city itself and his early experiences there influenced his mature poetry very deeply. There is an interesting exchange of letters with his friend Giordani which sums the matter up. Leopardi had written: "My homeland is Italy: I burn with love for her, thanking Heaven that I am an Italian." Giordani in his reply cleverly attempts to encourage Leopardi to love his native city by instancing the Piedmontese poet and dramatist Vittorio Alfieri, who was also born into an old aristocratic family and gave up his inheritance for the sake of physical and intellectual freedom, and who had died less than twenty years before:

> It seems to me that a wise man has to love his native region; and it seems to me that you have good reason to love your Recanati. Note that Alfieri, whom you justly admire, prided himself on his Asti – and Piedmont is no better than Piceno, or Recanati any worse than Asti.

Leopardi's reply has all his customary sharpness:

> It is well said: Plutarch and Alfieri loved Chaeronea and Asti. They loved them and they did not stay there. In the same way I shall still love my hometown when I am far away from it; now I say I hate it because I am living in it.

At all events, Giacomo's unhappiness did not prevent his years before he left Recanati from being extremely productive: at this early age he composed many of the finest poems in his *Canti*, including 'Bruto minore' ('Brutus'), 'Ultimo canto di Saffo' ('Sappho's Last Song'), 'L'infinito' ('The Infinite'), 'La sera del dì di festa' ('The Evening of the Holy Day') and 'Alla luna' ('To the Moon'); in 1817 he began his *Zibaldone* (*Commonplace Book*), the detailed notebook which he kept until the end of 1832, and also his short collection of aphorisms and general reflections, *Pensieri* (*Thoughts*), concerned mainly with social matters.

The topics covered in the *Zibaldone* are amazingly wide-ranging. The philological discussions are probably of interest to very few nowadays, and that interest must be mainly historical: as in any scientific study, even those suggestions on which future research can be based are then superseded. Nothing else in this work is ephemeral. This is a writer's notebook: the nearest thing we have to it in English for critical sharpness and discrimination is Coleridge's *Biographia Literaria*, which has a much narrower range and is a brilliant hotchpotch. Unlike Coleridge, Leopardi does not throw out intriguing suggestions which he promises to follow up and then fails to: he returns to topics again and again until his thoughts on them are exhausted. Except for a tendency to finish sentences with "etc.", as an indication that there is more to say on the subject, he does not write in note form. The result, since he even provided his own index to the book, is that it is easy to extract from it lengthy and coherent essays on very many topics. Even his discussion of what might appear at first a triviality treated in a pedantic manner – his preference for what he calls, from the Greek, *monofagia* ("eating alone") – reveals a sympathetic side of his character, is full of sound sense, and ultimately is concerned with civilized living. After first pointing out how the ancient Greeks and Romans thought this *monofagia* a sign of being "inhuman", Leopardi says:

I would have incurred this stigma among the ancients... But the ancients were right, because when they were at table together they talked only after they had eaten, when it was time for the symposium... time for drinking together, which they were accustomed to do after eating, as the English do today, to the accompaniment of at most a few titbits to stimulate their thirst. That was the time when they were more joyful, more lively, more spirited, more good-humoured, and had a greater wish to converse and chatter. But while they were eating they kept silent, or spoke very little. We have given up the natural and pleasant custom of drinking together, and we talk while we eat. Now I cannot convince myself that the one time of the day when we have our mouths full, when our external organs of speech are otherwise occupied (in an interesting task, and one which it is important to do well, because on a good digestion largely depends our well-being, our good physical, and hence also mental and moral, state – and our digestion cannot be good if it does not start well at the mouth...) should be precisely that time when we are more than ever obliged to speak; just because there are many people who, devoting for some reason or other all the rest of the day to study in retirement, only speak at mealtimes and would be quite angry to find themselves alone and having to stay silent at that time. But I, who have a good digestion much at heart, do not believe that I am being "inhuman" if at that time I have less desire to speak than ever, and if I therefore dine alone. All the more because I wish and need to be able to digest the food which is in my mouth, and not do as others do who often devour it, simply putting it into their mouths and gulping it down. If their stomachs are happy with that, it does not follow that mine has to be...

Four years before Giacomo's departure from Recanati, Monaldo invited Pietro Giordani to visit the family. It was particularly to this visit, and the influence of Giordani, twenty-four years older than Giacomo and strongly anti-clerical, that Monaldo attributed Giacomo's revolt against the values of his upbringing, and his alienation from his parents. This is to underestimate grossly Giacomo's own intelligence and determination. The letter in which Monaldo makes the complaint contains a sentence which, all unawares, reveals why Giacomo had to break away: "Until this day he had never, *literally never,* been one hour out of my sight or his mother's." This is only a slight exaggeration, for Carlo says that, until his walks with Giordani, Giacomo had never left the house unaccompanied by his tutor or by servants. After all, this was a twenty-year-old, whose father, incidentally, had come to his majority at the age of eighteen, and married at twenty-one.

Rome   Carlo Antici, the maternal uncle who had tried so hard in 1813 to have Giacomo live with him in Rome, and had been foiled by Monaldo, eventually succeeded nine years later. When he, along with others of his family, visited the Leopardis in Recanati, he was horrified to find how Giacomo's poor physical state had worsened, and he renewed his offer, which this time was accepted.

Carlo Antici's intention was the praiseworthy and common-sensical one of providing a sort of convalescence for his nephew, with occasional relief from his never-ending studies, and also the chance to widen his acquaintance. There was some immediate success: even the journey to Rome appeared to help, and there seems every reason to believe Giacomo's physical health did improve during his time in Rome. However, his psychological health was another matter, and he soon relapsed into his habitual melancholy: the rescue had come too late to change established habits.

88

Leopardi's letters now show a continuation of his habit of complaining, a habit which remained wherever he moved to. He had found the even tenor of life at Recanati stifling, but now he found the extremely uneven tenor of life in the turbulent household of Carlo Antici more than he could bear. He did not like the women he saw in Rome: one may surmise that he was not so fashioned as to make them like him. Even those scholars he met tended to disappoint him: their chief pursuits appeared to be archaeology and antiquarianism, which, Giacomo was not slow to point out, could make little progress among people whose knowledge of Latin and Greek was so inadequate. He even wrote to Paolina: "Be assured that the most stupid citizen of Recanati has more good sense than the wisest and most serious Roman." Were things really so bad? In a letter to Carlo he mentions refusing a chance of advancement because it entailed taking orders (which, given his opinion of religion, was obviously an honourable refusal); in the same letter, however, he admits: "...My happiness cannot consist in anything other than in doing what I want to do." With such an extreme requirement, it is hardly surprising that he was seldom happy anywhere.

Although he gained no employment, which would have made him his own master, and no happiness either, his time in Rome was nevertheless not wasted. As always, wherever he was, his comments on the city are worth noticing: they show once more that typical generalizing power of his, and they are relevant to every great city:

All the great size of Rome serves only to multiply the distances, and the number of steps to be climbed, when you wish to visit anyone. These immense buildings, and these con-sequently interminable streets, are so many spaces thrown between men, instead of being spaces which contain men.

All visitors to great cities go to see the sights, and Leopardi was no exception. Where he is an exception, however, is once again in his power to generalize from his experience, and generalize in such a way that we accept the truth of what he says, as we see in a letter to Carlo:

On Friday 15 February 1823 I went to visit the tomb of Tasso, and I wept over it. This is the first and only pleasure which

I have experienced in Rome. The way is long, and one only goes there in order to see this tomb; but who would not come even from America to enjoy the pleasure of tears for the space of two minutes? And it is most certain also that the immense expense I see people going to here, merely to get some pleasure or other, has the opposite result, because instead of pleasure they get nothing but boredom. Many people feel indignant when they see that Tasso's ashes are covered and marked by nothing but a stone, about a span and a half square, placed in one corner of a wretched little church. I would certainly not want to find these ashes in a mausoleum. You can imagine the mass of emotions which arise from thinking of the contrast between Tasso's greatness and his humble tomb. But you can have no idea of another contrast, that experienced by the eye which is accustomed to the infinite magnificence and vastness of the monuments in Rome, when it compares them with the smallness and bareness of this tomb. There is a sad and awesome consolation in thinking that this poverty is still able to interest and inspire posterity, while the superb mausoleums of Rome are observed with utter indifference to the people for whom they were raised, whose names are either not even asked, or else asked not as the names of people but as the names of monuments.

Return to Recanati Disappointed in Rome, there was nothing for it but to go back to Recanati in 1823, or in Leopardi's own words, "to return to the tomb". Here, with his health somewhat improved, he was able not only to continue writing his *Zibaldone,* but in one year, 1824, to compose the whole of his chief imaginative prose work, *Operette morali (Moral Fables).* A striking feature of this book is its revelation of a talent for comedy, which no one would have suspected from a reading of the *Canti* alone. With Leopardi criticism always goes hand in glove with creation, and he gives us a succinct *raison d'être* for the work, which has also a relevance to all comedy:

So that the ridiculous may be both worthwhile and also pleasing in a lively and lasting way – that is, so that it may not become boring – it must be applied to a serious and important matter... The more serious the subject matter is which is treated in a ridiculous manner, the more what is ridiculous becomes delightful, by means of the contrast etc.

The subject matter of the dialogues and fables, of which *Moral Fables* consists, could hardly be more serious, since it is the whole of human life and its purpose, or lack of it.

In May 1825 Leopardi went to Bologna on his way to *Bologna and Milan* Milan, in response to an invitation from the publisher Antonio Fortunato Stella, who wished for his collaboration in the publication of the entire works of Cicero in Latin, with the translation of a selection into Italian. Leopardi accepted gladly, once Stella had promised to pay his travelling expenses. When he set off, his eyes were giving him trouble, but once again leaving Recanati did him good, despite the rigours of the journey. His friend Giordani had been singing his praises, and he found himself among friends and admirers. He was so pleased with Bologna that he would have preferred to stay in that city, but he had to go on to Milan, where he remained less than a month (after writing to Carlo that one week's stay there would be unendurable), and then returned to Bologna, having agreed with Stella to continue his work on Cicero from there. Eventually Stella came to provide him with a monthly stipend which enabled him to continue to live away from his home in Recanati. While he was in Bologna, Leopardi, whose fame was growing, published a selection of his *Moral Fables*, and also completed a detailed commentary on Petrarch's *Canzoniere*.

From the time of his first infatuation with his father's cousin, Geltrude Cassi Lazzari, Giacomo had been well aware that his physique was not such as to inspire love in women, and he had determined to become famous so that he would be received by them with pleasure and esteem. In Bologna he made the acquaintance of Teresa Carniani Malvezzi, a countess with strong literary interests who had, when Leopardi met her in 1826, already published an Italian translation into blank verse of Pope's *Rape of the Lock*. A strong friendship grew up between them, which lasted for five or six months.

A brief return to his native city did nothing to arouse any *Florence* enthusiasm for it in Leopardi. When he returned to Bologna he did not see the Countess Malvezzi: she had asked him to visit her less frequently, and he had stopped visiting entirely. He was in that city only a couple of months in the summer of 1826, before going on to Florence.

Florence at this time was the most appealing place in Italy for one of Leopardi's outlook. The government was a comparatively liberal one, attracting intellectuals from all over the land. Gian Pietro Vieusseux, a Ligurian of Swiss descent, had founded in 1819 a Gabinetto Scientifico-Letterario (Scientific and Literary Society) in the very centre of the city, and this became a favourite meeting place for intellectuals. They were all united in their respect for *italianità*, their sense of the importance of the concept of Italy as a distinctive place and as a whole. In other matters their opinions might differ widely. The Marchese Gino Capponi, a member of one of the most illustrious families of Florence, a firm Catholic and a meliorist, was the man who had first suggested to Vieusseux the founding of a daily paper, the *Antologia*, to spread liberal opinions. Years later he was mercilessly mocked by Leopardi in his heavily ironical poem 'Palinodia al Marchese Gino Capponi' ('Palinode to the Marchese Gino Capponi'), simply because his views were seen by Leopardi as altogether too optimistic.

Publication of In the Palazzo Buondelmonti, the usual meeting place *Moral Fables* for these various men of letters, Leopardi met Alessandro Manzoni, whose *I promessi sposi* (*The Betrothed*) was published in the same year (1827) as Leopardi's *Moral Fables*, and both by the same publisher, Stella, in Milan. Manzoni wrote of Leopardi's work that "for its style, perhaps nothing better has been written in Italian in our time". Leopardi's first impressions of Manzoni's novel, after sampling a few pages, were not quite so enthusiastic, but when he read the work in full he recognized its quality. Whereas the first printing of *I promessi sposi* sold out in just over a month, the *Moral Fables* was much slower in making its way. The reason for this slowness is perhaps hinted at in Manzoni's praise above, and it became clear among the friends in Florence that, while Leopardi's style and élan were much appreciated, many found the sheer unrelenting pessimism of the work hard to take.

While he was in Florence Leopardi suffered continually with his eyes – to such an extent, indeed, that he said he could go out of doors only at night like a bat. Even so, he worked away at compiling an index to his *Zibaldone*. Despite his customary complaints – he told his sister Paolina for instance that in his lodgings "we pay a lot and eat little" – Leopardi was in many ways happier in Florence than he had been elsewhere, and he left the city in the late autumn of 1827 only in order to spend the winter in a place where the climate was milder.

His chosen place of refuge was Pisa. Although a friend *Pisa*
affirmed later that he had never seen Leopardi smile even once
while he was there, in Pisa he seems to have been immediately
happy:

I am enchanted with Pisa because of the climate: if it lasts
like this, it will be heaven. I left Florence one degree above
freezing; here I have found so much warmth that I have had to
cast my cloak off and wear lighter clothing. The appearance
of Pisa pleases me much more than that of Florence. The
road by the side of the Arno here forms a spectacle so vast,
so magnificent, so gay, so charming, that it makes one fall in
love with it; I have seen nothing like it in Florence or Milan
or Rome – and truly I do not know whether in the whole of
Europe many such sights can be found. And it is very pleasant
to stroll there in the winter, because the air is almost always
springlike: so that at certain hours of the day that district is
full of people, full of carriages and pedestrians; ten or twenty
languages can be heard, and bright sunshine glitters on the
gilding of the cafés, the shops full of bijouterie, and the
windows of the palaces and houses, all the fine architecture.
And for the rest, Pisa is a mixture of big town and little town,
of urban and rural, a mixture so romantic that I have never
seen anything like it.

This passage is from a letter to Paolina. It is interesting that
very many years later, when Giacomo was long dead and
when Paolina was able, for the first time in her life, to venture
beyond Recanati, she chose to go to Pisa and recalled this
letter as what inspired her to go there.

While he was in the city he wrote 'Il risorgimento' ('The
Revival') and 'A Silvia' ('To Silvia'). If it is true, as most
scholars think, that the latter commemorates Teresa Fattorini,
the daughter of the coachman in Leopardi's childhood home,
then the poem must have been incubating for a decade: it
is an instance of his method of working that the poem was
written only when its subject matter was so well digested that
its general significance was clear. 'A Silvia' is noteworthy also
as the first of his poems to use a form of verse which, although
tightly controlled and rhymed, was not composed on a regular
pattern. Many other poems – including 'Canto notturno di
un pastore errante dell'Asia' ('Night Song of a Wandering

93

Shepherd of Asia'), 'La quiete dopo la tempesta' ('The Calm
after the Storm'), and 'Il sabato del villaggio' ('The Village
Saturday') – follow this precedent.

Leopardi felt so much better generally when he was in Pisa
that he was at this time able to look forward to his old age (an
old age that in fact he never reached) with a certain mellow
equanimity and pleasure even:

> One of the most important results that I intend and hope
> will come from my verses, is that they should heat my old
> age with the warmth of my youth; that I should savour them
> at that time, and experience some vestige of my past feelings,
> placed there to preserve them and make them last, as if on
> deposit; that I should be moved as I reread them, as often
> happens with me, and more than in reading other people's
> poetry; that they should make me not only remember, but
> also reflect on what I was, and compare myself with myself;
> and finally that they should give me the pleasure one feels in
> enjoying and appreciating one's own works, and seeing for
> oneself and delighting in the beauties and merits of one's
> own son, with no other satisfaction than that of having
> brought something beautiful into the world; whether it is
> recognized as such by other people or not.

In May 1828 his brother Luigi died at the age of twenty-four,
but Leopardi did not go immediately to Recanati to be with
his family. He cited health reasons for his absence. In June
he returned to Florence. There he received a letter from Karl
Bunsen, the Prussian ambassador to the Vatican, whom he
had first met some years previously in Rome. The letter offered
him the Chair of Dante Studies in Bonn, in terms which were
not only flatteringly persuasive but also showed a knowledge
of how Leopardi might best be persuaded:

> There in Bonn, in a climate like that of Verona, with winters
> in which the temperature rarely drops below 4° Réaumur
> when it is cold, you would be surrounded by learned friends
> and a zealous crowd anxious to see the Chair of Dante
> revived beyond the Alps.

Even though this appointment would have removed his money
problems and made him independent, Leopardi refused the

offer – finding himself unable to leave Italy and his family behind and, despite the assurances, fearful of the climate in Germany.

In November 1828 Leopardi, unable to support himself financially any longer away from home, returned to Recanati for what was to be his last visit to his hometown. He did not find any reason to rejoice there. First there was the mourning for his brother Luigi, in which Giacomo joined, for his filial and familial piety was strong, even if he so often resented it in himself. A further cause of distress was the estrangement that had developed between his brother Carlo and their parents. Carlo had fallen in love with a young cousin without a dowry, and was determined to marry her, while his parents were negotiating what they considered a better match with another young cousin who had a dowry. The matter was settled, although not amicably, when Carlo took advantage of his father's temporary absence from home to get married.

Another Stay in Recanati

Giacomo, as always, was anxious to get away, apparently at any cost, as a letter to Vieusseux explains:

I am resolved, with the little money which I have from when I was able to work, to set out on my travels in search of either health or death, and never again return to Recanati. I do not mind what sort of work I do: anything which is compatible with my state of health will suit me. I shall not be afraid of humiliation, because there is no humiliation or discouragement greater than that I suffer now living in this centre of European barbarism and ignorance.

At the same time, we have already seen how he tended to refuse good offers of employment; moreover, it was not easy to see what work would be compatible with his state of health. At times it seemed to him that he would never leave Recanati, but die there. However, extreme unhappiness did not destroy his creativity: 'Le ricordanze' ('Remembrances'), 'Canto notturno di un pastore errante dell'Asia', 'La quiete dopo la tempesta', and 'Il sabato del villaggio' were all composed during his short last visit of sixteen months to Recanati.

Rescue came in a way and a manner which he could accept. His friend Pietro Colletta, the Neapolitan historian, wrote to him from Florence of a subsidy which had been arranged for Leopardi's subsistence in the Tuscan city. Colletta gave himself out to be merely the agent in the matter, while the money came from anonymous donors. The subsidy lasted, as had been promised, for a year. It was probably the fact that only the small group of anonymous donors would know of his straitened circumstances and need for charity which induced Leopardi to accept, but sheer desperation may also have played a part.

Return to Florence   In Florence, where Leopardi arrived in May 1830, he did at last think that he was receiving his due as a writer. It was there that the first edition of his *Canti* was published, but even before that a letter to Paolina, sent with a portrait of himself, betrays an unwonted sense of satisfaction:

> This portrait of me is very ugly: let it nevertheless be passed about down there, so that the inhabitants of Recanati may see with their physical eyes (which are the only ones they have) that "the Leopardis' hunchback" counts for something in the world, where Recanati is not known even by name.

There was also a final affair of the heart, if that is the right description for an idealistic and platonic friendship with a married woman, Fanny Targioni Tozzetti, which did not – indeed by its nature could not – lead to anything more intimate. However, the most important event in Leopardi's life at this time was the renewal and strengthening of his acquaintance with Antonio Ranieri, the best friend he ever had.

Antonio Ranieri   Ranieri was a Neapolitan, eight years younger than Leopardi, who had first met him three years previously. He was travelling for his education, supported financially by his father in Naples. Suspected of being that dangerous thing, "a liberal", he knew that, if he returned to Naples, he might well not be allowed to leave it again, and so he continued travelling, not visiting his hometown even when his mother died. He seems to have visited Leopardi at this time in Florence out of pity, but that developed into a companionship of seven years, no less important for the fact that they seemed to have so little in common.

Brief Stay in Rome   In October 1831 Ranieri went to Rome to be close to an actress with whom he was smitten. Leopardi also went to Rome, for what turned out to be only a few months, because he did not wish to be parted from Ranieri. They took lodgings together there, as they had latterly in Florence, and apart from a brief visit of Ranieri's to Bologna, they lived together for the rest of Giacomo's life.

It was while Leopardi was back in Florence in early 1832 that there occurred a rare comical interlude. Towards the end of 1831 his father had published a work evincing extremely conservative religious and political opinions, *Dialoghetti sulle materie correnti nell'anno 1831* (*Short Dialogues on Current Affairs in the Year 1831*), and it was generally believed to be the work of Giacomo, and therefore to represent an astonishing change of heart. His response to the rumours – in a letter to his cousin Giuseppe Melchiorri – was forthright:

> My father himself will think it only just that I refuse to usurp the glory which is due to him... I do not wish to be seen any more with the blot on my honour of having produced that infamous, most infamous, most wicked book. Here everyone thinks that it is mine: that is because the author is Leopardi, my father is unknown and I am known, and therefore I am the author... In Milan they are saying openly that I am the author, that I have been converted just as Monti was.

The versatility, or adaptability to every changing requirement, *Naples* shown by the poet Vincenzo Monti was abhorrent to Leopardi.

In September 1833 Leopardi set off for Naples. In a letter to his father, explaining why he did not go to Recanati, he claimed that Naples would be better for his health, especially during the winter. He travelled with Ranieri, who was no longer afraid of returning to his native city. They arrived at the beginning of October, and first impressions were favourable:

> I got here satisfactorily, that is without harm and without accidents. On the other hand my health is not very good, and my eyes are still in the same condition. However, I like very much the mildness of the climate, the beauty of the city, and the lovable and kindly disposition of the inhabitants.

A year or so later his opinion seems to have changed:

> ...I can no longer endure this half-barbarous and half-African place, where I live in complete isolation from everyone.

That comment is also from a letter to his father, to whom he was almost obliged to express a longing for Recanati, so its sincerity is hard to judge. There are, however, other letters expressing the same dislike of Naples and its citizens. He did have various schemes for moving elsewhere, and it is likely that Ranieri did not encourage them since he himself was at home in Naples, but to some extent this is the same old story wherever he was. Moreover, he was not "living in complete isolation": there was companionship and help from Ranieri's family, especially Ranieri's sister Paolina, who eventually acted as Leopardi's nurse. His health did improve in the southern climate. Perhaps the truth is that he was not meeting friends with the same intellectual and artistic interests as himself, and his health, however improved, was still bad. As always, he went on writing. He produced in these years more poems for the *Canti*, including 'Sopra un basso rilievo antico sepolcrale, dove una giovane morta è rappresentata in atto di partire, accommiatandosi dai suoi' ('Upon a Bas-relief on an Ancient Tomb Showing a Dead Girl in the Act of Departing and Taking Leave of Her Family'), 'Sopra il ritratto di una bella donna scolpito nel monumento sepolcrale della medesima' ('On the Likeness of a Beautiful Lady Carved upon her Tomb'), 'Aspasia' and 'La ginestra, o il fiore del deserto' ('The Broom, or the Flower of the Desert').

Ranieri's Memoirs   Leopardi's habit of complaining, which was a way of life with him, had in Naples an effect that was very unfortunate for some involved, but also valuable for the provision of important biographical details. Long after his death some of his letters were published and revealed his adverse opinion of Naples and the Neapolitans. Understandably, Ranieri, now an old man, was upset by these revelations and in 1880, to put the matter straight, he published his *Sette anni di sodalizio con Giacomo Leopardi* (*Seven Years' Companionship with Giacomo Leopardi*). The result has been a general vilification of Ranieri: he wrote to justify himself and his sister (since he appeared to think they were included in his friend's attacks on the Neapolitans), and his justification is couched in terms too excessive to be quite believable. He exaggerated the scale of Leopardi's financial dependence on him, and there are apparently other lies or false memories. These charges may all be true, but it is not difficult to defend Ranieri. He went to Florence when he believed his friend was near death, settled his affairs in that city for him, took him with him to Naples, settled him down there, with the help of his own friends and relatives, and nursed him for years and during his final illness. Leopardi cannot have been an easy patient. It should be borne in mind also that Ranieri was not a professional writer and, if he misjudged the right tone for his own defence, that should not blind us to the good he did do. To complain that he tells us about Leopardi's ice-cream habit, but does not record any conversations on artistic or intellectual matters, saying, as one critic has, that he was no Eckermann or Boswell, is grossly unfair. Ranieri dwelt on the harsh, even sordid, facts of looking after a seriously sick man, and that is not surprising, since it is what he had to deal with. Everyone wonders what Ranieri and Leopardi saw in each other, since they seemed to have so little in common: perhaps Leopardi found it relaxing to be with someone who did not question him and badger him *à la* Eckermann or Boswell. Ranieri did preserve three striking additions to the Leopardi poetical canon – 'Il tramonto della luna', 'La ginestra', and two extra and essential lines for 'Alla luna' – which would otherwise have remained unknown; he also produced the first complete edition of the *Canti* in 1845.

To Ranieri we owe also a first-hand account of Leopardi's *Death* death which, professional writer or not, is very affecting and informative:

The soup was already served. He had come to the table more cheerful than usual, and had already taken two or three spoonfuls, when turning to me, who was by his side:

"I feel my asthma getting a bit worse," he said (for so he persisted in calling what were obviously symptoms of his illness): "could we have the doctor back?"

This was Professor Niccolò Mannella, who had been the most assiduous and the most affectionate of his doctors, a man of remarkable knowledge and of even more remarkable integrity, the regular doctor to the Royal Prince of Salerno.

"And why not?" I replied. "In fact I'll go for him myself."

It was one of those days memorable for the number of deaths from cholera, and it did not seem to me a time to be sending messengers.

I think that, despite all my efforts, a little of the deep perturbation I felt must have shown in my face. Because he got up and joked about it and smiled; clasping my hand,

99

he reminded me that asthmatics were long-lived. I left in the very carriage which had been waiting to take us away [for an excursion into the country]. I entrusted him to my people, and especially to my sister Paolina, his usual attendant and nurse whom he rewarded so generously when he used to say that only his Paolina of Naples enabled him to bear the great distance from his Paolina of Recanati.

I found Mannella at home, and he dressed and came with me. But everything had changed. So used was our beloved patient to long and painful deadly illnesses, and so accustomed to frequent intimations of death, that he could no longer distinguish the true symptoms of it from the false. And not really shaken in his faith that his illness was wholly nervous, he had a blind confidence in being able to alleviate it with food. So that, despite the fervent entreaties of the bystanders, he had tried three times to rise from the bed on which they had laid him fully dressed as he was, and three times he had tried to sit at the table again to have his lunch. But each time, after a few sips, he had been forced, despite himself, to desist and go back to bed – where, when I arrived with Mannella, we found him not lying down, but merely on the edge of the bed, with some pillows across it to support him.

He cheered up when we arrived and smiled at us, and although his voice was somewhat fainter and more faltering than usual, he argued gently with Mannella about his nervous ailment, his certainty of alleviating it with food, how he was bored with ass's milk, of the wonders brought about by excursions and his wish now to get up and go into the countryside. But Mannella, deftly taking me aside, advised me to send at once for a priest, since there was no time for anything else. And I sent immediately, and again and yet again, to the nearest monastery of the Discalced Augustinians.

In the meantime – while we were all round him, with Paolina supporting his head and drying the sweat which poured down from that broad forehead of his, and with me, seeing him overtaken by an ominous and mysterious stupor, trying to rouse him with various kinds of smelling salts – Leopardi opened his eyes wider than usual, and stared at me more fixedly than ever. Then:

"I can't see you any more," he said to me with a sigh.
And he stopped breathing: neither pulse nor heart was
beating any more. At that very moment Brother Felice
of St Augustine, a Discalced Augustinian, came in: while
I, beside myself, was calling in a loud voice to my friend
and brother and father, who did not answer me any more,
although he still seemed to be looking at me.

Leopardi's old friend Pietro Giordani provided his epitaph:

TO THE MEMORY OF COUNT GIACOMO LEOPARDI OF RECANATI
PHILOLOGIST ADMIRÈD BEYOND ITALY
ILLUSTRIOUS PHILOSOPHER AND POET
COMPARABLE ONLY TO THE GREEKS
WHO DIED AT THE AGE OF THIRTY-NINE
AFTER SEVERE AND UNREMITTING ILL HEALTH
THIS STONE WAS LAID BY ANTONIO RANIERI
WHO FOR SEVEN YEARS UNTIL THE FINAL HOUR
WAS WITH HIS BELOVED FRIEND
MDCCCXXXVII

Giacomo's sister Paolina noted the death in the family
records:

On the fourteenth day of June 1837 there died in the city of
Naples this dear brother of mine who had become one of
the foremost men of letters in Europe. He was buried in the
church of San Vitale, on the Via di Pozzuoli. Farewell, dear
Giacomo. When shall we meet again in Paradise?

There is a sour footnote to these accounts. In 1900, when the
tomb was opened up, the paucity of human remains found
in it suggested that Ranieri had told another lie (since this
could scarcely be something he misremembered) when he
said that he had saved his friend's body from being thrown
into a common grave, the usual fate of those who died
during the cholera epidemic of 1837. If so, it was surely a
kindly lie.
In 1937, the centenary of Leopardi's death, his presumed
remains were transferred from San Vitale to the Virgilian Park
at Piedigrotta to rest near the tomb of Virgil.

Leopardi's Works

Juvenilia Although Leopardi died young, at the age of thirty-nine, his literary career spans nearly thirty years. In 1808, when only ten, he was required to make a presentation to his family to show what he had learnt. Before the age of eleven he had composed his first poem, the sonnet 'La morte di Ettore' ('The death of Hector'), and he had even translated the first two books of Horace's *Odes*.

1809 saw the beginning of his years of "mad and desperate study". During this time he produced many works, including a translation of Horace's *Ars Poetica* into *ottava rima*, a tragedy in three acts, *La virtù indiana* (*The Indian Virtue*), and another tragedy, *Pompeo in Egitto* (*Pompey in Egypt*). At the age of fifteen, when he began his study of ancient Greek (without a tutor), he wrote his *Storia dell'astronomia* (*History of Astronomy*). In the following years he made many translations from the Greek.

Other translations, poems, essays and tragedies followed, and many interesting letters, the earliest of which to survive with a date was written in December 1810, and the last in May 1837, only a couple of weeks before his death. It would serve no purpose to try to list all of Leopardi's writings here, but it is worth noting that the complete works edited by Walter Binni and Enrico Ghidetti in 1969, in two volumes, consist of nearly 3,000 pages in smallish print with double columns. Despite the quality of so many of his lesser works, Leopardi's fame rests squarely on three separate large-scale achievements – his *Canti*, his *Moral Fables* and his *Zibaldone*.

Canti The earliest poem to be included in the *Canti* dates from 1816, and two of the poems were written almost twenty years later. The contents show, not surprisingly, various levels of poetic maturity, obscured somewhat by the fact that in the *Canti* the contents are not arranged chronologically. There were several partial editions in Leopardi's lifetime, culminating in one in 1835 – the last to receive his direct attention – which contained all the *Canti* as we now have them with the exception of 'Il tramonto della luna', 'La ginestra' and lines 13–14 of 'Alla luna'. These were included in Antonio Ranieri's posthumous edition of 1845, which there is every reason to believe followed Leopardi's wishes: all subsequent editions are ultimately based on this one.

Leopardi is one of those poets who seem to tempt their critics to discuss their "ideas" rather than the poetry itself. This may well be because the verse in which the ideas are expressed is so accomplished, so apparently simple that, while giving its reader great pleasure and satisfaction, it gives a literary critic little to talk about. What is expressed in a poem matters, of course, but we must always remember what Mallarmé said to Degas: poems are made not with ideas but with words.

Leopardi's poems are crystal-clear; indeed, to a modern reader his refusal to be oblique can at times be quite shocking. The poems frequently express the most common of commonplaces:

The happiest days
Of our allotted time are first to go.
Disease succeeds, and old age, and the shadow
Of chilly death.
['Sappho's Last Song', 65–68]

A much more complex reflection may be expressed even more simply:

If life is all so dire,
Why do we still endure?
['Night Song', 55–56]

If the sheer simplicity of what Leopardi says, and how he says it, may puzzle the critic and baffle the translator, the nature of what he says seems to affront many others. In an age like ours which often seems to pride itself on its ability to "take a full look at the worst" – when only unhappiness is news and an autobiography is nothing without a troubled childhood – it is fascinating to see people flinch from Leopardi's outlook and concentrate instead on what they think might have caused his apparent pessimism. If it can all be put down to his poor state of health, the hunch on his back and his generally unhappy life, then he can be accommodated in a slot already available in the mind as another Romantic *poète maudit*. And then his poems become mere symptoms of a disease, and so much the less valuable as poems. He foresaw this very clearly, and protested against it:

103

> My feelings towards destiny have been and still are those which I expressed in 'Brutus'... being led by my researches to a philosophy of despair, I did not hesitate to embrace it fully; while on the other hand it is only because of the cowardice of men, who need to be persuaded that existence is worthwhile, that people have wanted to consider my philosophical opinions the result of my personal sufferings, and that they persist in attributing to my physical condition what comes only from my understanding. Before I die I am going to protest against this invention of weakness and vulgarity, and ask my readers to apply themselves to destroying my observations and arguments rather than to blaming my illnesses.

It is obvious that Leopardi does in his poetry and elsewhere speak frequently about himself, and also about his family, but this is never merely for the sake of speaking about himself. One of the observations in his *Zibaldone* is quite typical, in its small way, of his normal procedure:

> My mother once said to Pietrino, who was weeping for an old stick of his which had been thrown out of the window by Luigi: "Don't cry, don't cry: I would have thrown it out anyway." And he was consoled because he would have lost it in any case.

The consolation to be obtained from lack of hope is ubiquitous in his poetry. Other personal details, when they appear, are similarly generalized.

Leopardi can deal interestingly with contemporary social matters, as he shows particularly in his *Thoughts*, but in his poetry he is most effective when his generalities are concerned with matters beyond the merely contemporary and social. For instance, after a description of Christopher Columbus's discoveries there is a comment, not on one man's foolish optimism, but the general and unavoidable metaphysical disillusionment of all men:

> But the discovered world
> Does not increase – it shrinks; so much more vast
> The sounding air, the fertile earth, the seas

Seem to the child than to the man who knows.
['To Angelo Mai', 87–90]

The subject is ultimately almost always metaphysical – the meaning of life itself. We see this again in a meditation which begins with the lava-covered slopes of Mount Vesuvius:

Often, on these bare slopes
Clothed in a kind of mourning
By stone waves which apparently still ripple,
I sit by night, and see the distant stars
High in the clear blue sky
Flame down upon this melancholy waste,
And see them mirrored by
The distant sea, till all this universe
Sparkles throughout its limpid emptiness.
['The Broom', 158–66]

In both those passages Leopardi is prompted to his meditation by important matters – in the first by Angelo Mai's discovery of some lost books of Cicero, which leads to a consideration of a different kind of discovery, and thence to Everyman's exploration of the world in which he has to live and his disillusionment; in the second the prompting comes from the contemplation of Vesuvius and its destructive power. Such important matters – or others, like the always impressive sight of the moon, or the premature death of a young girl – might lead anyone to wonder about humanity's *raison d'être*, but often with Leopardi the spur is something in itself trivial – a singing thrush, the looking forward to a holy day, the end of a holy day, the relief when a storm blows itself out. In such poems, even when the subject matter at first seems to be quite personal, the real subject is the metaphysical question of humankind's destiny and place in the world. Again, in 'The Evening of the Holy Day', lament for the ending of a festival modulates into lament for the transitoriness of everything, and it is that which is the true subject of the poem and gives it its power.

This is why the descriptions in Leopardi's poems tend to be generic and even vague: they are there not for themselves, as they well might be in many another poet, but for the thoughts they inspire: to go into detailed description would detract from this. We might say that Leopardi evokes, rather than celebrates, the countryside, and then not for its own sake.

If Leopardi's poetry is not notable for precise descriptions – such as an English reader finds so attractive in, to mention only poets of Leopardi's own century, Wordsworth, Keats, Tennyson and Hopkins – and if so much of his poetry consists of apparently simple statement, then where does its virtue lie? One answer is suggested by the fact that, although he shows no sharp visual sense, his hearing is acute. Time and again his meditations are provoked by sounds – of church bells, the wind, the rain, the song of birds, people whistling or singing by themselves, or shotguns being fired in celebration of a holy day. And this sensitivity to sound is apparent in the texture of his lines. This is most obvious when there is a gentle onomatopoeic effect:

> A gust of wind brings down the sounding hour
> From the tower of this town.
> ['Remembrances', 50–1]

Even more effective is when the sound of the line is devoted to an effect which is quite abstract, as in the last line here, with its feline movement:

> ...and [you] see what fruit
> Morning and evening bring,
> The silent and unending stealth of time.
> ['Night Song', 70-2]

There are even such effects where we might expect the resulting impression to be primarily a visual one. The strange caressing note of the second line here has often been noted:

> The countryside clears up,
> The river in the vale is visible.
> ['The Calm after the Storm', 6–7]

Very frequently the strong effect of lines making simple statements, and composed of simple, although often archaic words comes from the careful management of the syntax. Leopardi makes full use of – sometimes even stretches in a

106

rather Latinate way – the greater scope there is in Italian than in English for varying the position of words and particularly building up powerful periodic sentences, where no word is used until it can appear at its most effective.

Leopardi's customary clarity does not mean that he is a poet where strong clear statement is all. Far from it: he is frequently capable of effects which echo in the mind in that inexplicable and eerie way which we think of as especially Romantic. One such effect can be obtained by a rapid movement over long stretches of time. We find this in one of Shakespeare's sonnets when, after expressing his fear that his friend's beauty, which seems unchanging, may be decaying, he says, addressing us four hundred years later:

> For fear of which hear this, thou age unbred:
> Ere you were born was beauty's summer dead.

There is a similar effect, but now going back in time, at the end of 'The Eve of St Agnes', when Keats, after describing the lovers' elopement in such a way as to make it seem as though it is happening before our very eyes, says:

> And they are gone: aye, ages long ago
> These lovers fled away into the storm.

In 'The Evening of the Holy Day', after moving from the sadness at the end of the present holy day to the disappearance of the ancient Romans, Leopardi comes back, not to the present, but first to his own past, before returning to the present which, the final image implies, is itself fast disappearing:

> All is at peace all silent through their world,
> And nowadays we hardly talk of them.
> In my first age, that age when holy days
> Are desperately desired, then I remember,
> A holy day once gone, I lay awake
> In pain though feather-bedded; and late at night
> A song I chanced to hear along the paths
> Dying into the distance bit by bit
> In this way then as now clutched at my heart.
> [38–46]

This is not just an isolated effect in Leopardi: it is widespread. It strongly suggests what is often taken as his last word on the subject of human life:

> ...all the emptiness of everything.
> ['To Himself', 16]

Moral Fables Similarly to the Canti, the *Moral Fables* went through several editions in Leopardi's lifetime, with continual accretions. Its early history was only concluded after eighteen years by the posthumous edition published, by Ranieri once more, in 1845.

Laughter is not a word that usually springs to mind when we think of Leopardi. True, it would be tempting fate to assert that there is no humour in all the very many pages of the *Zibaldone*, but it is hard to remember any. In the *Canti* the heavy irony of 'Palinode to the Marchese Gino Capponi' is the nearest we come to wit or humour, and some may argue that does not come very near. But the *Moral Fables*, a slighter work than Leopardi's other two masterpieces, besides revealing Leopardi's gift for brief narrative, is a book full of witty turns – some cruel and some kind – and occasional broad genial humour.

The humour can be sardonic, as in this conversation between a visiting celebrity and a cannibal:

> PROMETHEUS: What nice kinds of food do you have?
> SAVAGE: This bit of meat.
> PROMETHEUS: Is that farmed meat or game?
> SAVAGE: Farmed. In fact it's my son...
> PROMETHEUS: Are you serious? You are eating your own flesh?
> SAVAGE: Not my own flesh, but this fellow's: it's the only reason I brought him into the world and took such care to nourish him.

There is also the ending of 'Nature and an Icelander', when a discussion of the nature of reality, anguished on the part of the Icelander and adamant on the part of Nature, is cut short by the sudden appearance of a man-eating lion, which promptly does what man-eating lions do and thus clinches the argument.

Often the humour is very gentle and gently refreshing, as it is throughout 'Prizes Offered by the Satirographical Academy', based as this is upon one simple incongruity – imagining that machines can take the place of people. In the dialogue 'A Pedlar of Almanacs and a Passer-by', we are all the object of genial humour – the naive seller of almanacs who appears to be oblivious throughout to what is going on, the traveller (representing Leopardi himself) who laughs at the seller's sales talk but ends up buying an almanac, and we readers who cannot help but recognize ourselves as just as foolish as those two. The humour here is kindly, even though it comes from the sheer frustration in the nature of things. Even in 'Frederick Ruysch and His Mummies', whose tone is overwhelmingly macabre, comedy is not far away.

All this is not to suggest that the *Moral Fables* are one long laugh. Although any reader coming to these fables after Leopardi's *Canti* is likely to be very often surprised at their tone, which can appear light-hearted, he would recognize the same general, and generally pessimistic, obsessions as in all of Leopardi's work – the impossibility of true happiness in this world or the next, the insubstantiality of human ideals of behaviour and the pervasive cruelty of Nature to her offspring. Leopardi has not changed his mind, but only his tone of voice. There must be few critics now who would agree with Edmund Wilson (in *Axel's Castle*) that "Leopardi is a sick man and... all his thinking is sick": that naive equation of a man with his work is long out of fashion. But it is a pleasure to watch "the Leopardis' hunchback" (as he saw himself in the eyes of his fellow citizens of Recanati) being, with all his unhappiness, not only energetic in his writing, but positively athletic.

The title *Thoughts* leads one to expect aphorisms and wit. *Thoughts* There is certainly no shortage of either. A good example of both is the sentence at the end of section 31: "Men are wretched by necessity, and determined to believe themselves wretched by accident". That statement, however, is the summary of a discussion which starts simply from noticing one of the common habits of mankind, and its full force is only evident when we read it at the end of that discussion. Unlike many writers of aphorisms, Leopardi does not parade his wit. It would be a mistake to skim through his writings in order to pick out the gems. Gems there are, but they are found scattered, apparently naturally, almost it would seem inevitably, in discussions which are comparatively lengthy and which frequently originate in some, at first trivial, observation.

The tone of this work, and an implicit suggestion as to how we should read it, is evident at its very beginning:

> For a long time I have denied the truth of the things I am about to say, because, apart from the fact that they are utterly foreign to my nature (and we always tend to judge others by ourselves), I have never been inclined to hate people, but to love them. In the end experience has persuaded, indeed almost forced me to believe the truth of these things.

This is a not a mere rhetorical flourish. As we read, we see Leopardi developing his thoughts in such a way that we are carried along with them and are ourselves frequently "persuaded, indeed almost forced" to accept the conclusion at the end of the line of argument. The result, then, is not a display of fireworks so much as a bright steady light illuminating the deeper significance of the most trivial human affairs.

It is, in keeping with the generalizing tendency of this whole work, not usual for Leopardi to include any personal details. He is thinking around things which we have all noticed, and personal details would merely intrude. It is significant that the "little boy" of section 90 was originally, in the source passage from the *Zibaldone*, "one of my brothers". Similarly, one cannot help believing that, had Leopardi himself lived to see *Thoughts* through the press, the details concerning Ranieri in section 4 would have been omitted and the protagonist of that story would have been simply "a young man". The common twenty-first century tendency to read, or rather misread, writers by moving from the work to the writer's life and being, rather than outward to the world, is a danger of which Leopardi was always aware and fought against, as we have seen before. When the writer is a chronically sick hunchback, known to have a difficult relationship with his family and many of those around him, and is distrusted for his "views", then the danger of this trivializing misreading is very great.

If the work were all in one key, then it would inevitably seem more personal than Leopardi intends. But it is not. Among the many sharp, indeed cutting, comments on social behaviour, there is, for instance, the discussion of anniversaries in section 13, which is humane and understanding in its vision of human frailties and suffering. As another example of the variety of the work, there is the long comic account (in section 20) of "the vice of reading or performing one's own compositions in front of others", which in itself contains great variety of tone. The modest proposal to cure this vice, with which the discussion ends, is, in its detailed ingenuity and in the poker face with which it is presented, most reminiscent to English readers of Jonathan Swift.

The reader who is familiar with Leopardi's other works will notice in *Thoughts* a rather different emphasis. The best of his poems, and most of his *Moral Fables*, are concerned with the cardinal feature that all that we value in this world, or in a putative other world, is illusory. Leopardi's *Thoughts* do not usually speak so directly of this ultimate emptiness, being concerned more with human beings in their social life, but it can often be sensed at the back of what he is saying. We see this in section 29, when he remarks, "Imposture is the soul, so to speak, of social life," but then moves to the clearly metaphysical conclusion: "Nature herself is an impostor towards man, making his life lovable and endurable principally by means of imagination and deception."

An example of the interpenetration of the two worlds, the social and the metaphysical, in *Thoughts* is Leopardi's quite frequent use of the term "the world", as when he says in the first section, "I maintain that the world is a league of scoundrels against honest men, and of the contemptible against the high-minded." Leopardi, who rejected both the Enlightenment belief in progress which was fashionable in his day and the Christianity in which he was brought up, shows the influence of the former in the fierceness with which he continually rejected it, but the influence of the latter in more complex ways. He acknowledges quite explicitly (in section 84) the source of the expression "the world" in the gospels, and in many respects the values which he opposes to "the world" are Christian. It would, of course, be absurd to suggest that Leopardi was a believer, but the surprising thing is the moral fervour he shows in treating of a world which he thinks of as an illusion. Beneath the surface clarity and ease of reading there is a surprisingly complex set of attitudes, and nothing can do justice to them but a sympathetic reading of the work itself.

Zibaldone   The *Zibaldone* (*Commonplace Book*) was, like Canti and
Moral Fables, also composed over a long period: Leopardi
first began to collect his scattered notes in the summer of
1817, and the last entry in the book is dated December 1832.
The 4,526 handwritten pages were included, after Leopardi's
death, by his executor, the notary Alessandro delli Ponti, in his
inventory of the writer's effects. The book was published sixty
years later, in six volumes which appeared from 1898 to 1900
under the title *Pensieri di varia filosofia e di bella letteratura
(Various Philosophical and Literary Thoughts)*, edited by a
team presided over by the poet and critic Giosuè Carducci.
Several selections from it followed; a further complete edition,
more carefully edited than Carducci's, appeared in 1937, when
it had the title *Zibaldone*, by which it is now known both in
Italian and in English. This too is a large-scale work which is
important in its own right. Unlike many writers' notebooks,
it is easy to use, being provided with indexes by Leopardi
himself and by his editors. Even if one discounts the purely
philological sections, *Zibaldone* contains far more material
than most readers can digest in their lifetime. It is difficult to
think of a comparable work anywhere.

– J.G. Nichols

Select Bibliography

Texts used for the translations in this edition:
Giacomo Leopardi, *Canti*, ed. Giuseppe and Domenico De
Robertis (Milan: Arnoldo Mondadori, 1978)
Giacomo Leopardi, *Operette morali*, ed. Cesare Galimberti,
3rd edn. (Naples: Guida Editori, 1988)
Giacomo Leopardi, *Pensieri* in *Tutte le opere*, ed. Walter
Binni and Enrico Ghidetti, 4th edn., vol. 1 (Florence: Sansoni,
1985).
Giacomo Leopardi *Zibaldone di Pensieri*, ed. Giuseppe
Pacella, 3 vols. (Milan: Garzanti, 1991)

Biographies:
Chiarini, Giuseppe *Vita di Giacomo Leopardi* (Rome:
Editrice Gela, 1921 – originally published 1905)
Iris Origo, *Leopardi: A Study in Solitude* (London: Hamish
Hamilton, 1953)
Album Leopardi (Milan: Arnoldo Mondadori, 1993). The

text, by Rolando Damiani, is in Italian; the book is lavishly and clearly illustrated.

Criticism:
J.H. Whitfield, *Giacomo Leopardi* (Oxford: Basil Blackwell, 1954). The best discussion of Leopardi's work as a whole.
J.H. Whitfield Alberti, *Leopardi and the Modus Morendi* (privately printed, October 1988)
Giovanni Carsaniga *Giacomo Leopardi: The Unheeded Voice* (Edinburgh: Edinburgh University Press, 1977)

Translations:
Geoffrey L. Bickersteth, *The Poems of Leopardi. Edited with Introduction and Notes and a Verse Translation in the Metres of the Original* (Cambridge: Cambridge University Press, 1923)
John Heath-Stubbs, *Collected Poems* (Manchester: Carcanet Press, 1988). This contains translations of eighteen of Leopardi's poems.
Leopardi: A Scottis Quair, ed. R.D.S. Jack, M.L. McLaughlin, and C. Whyte (Edinburgh University Press, 1987). This contains the Italian texts of twelve poems, with translations into English, Scots and Gaelic.
J.G. Nichols, *Giacomo Leopardi: The Canti with a selection of his prose* (Manchester: Carcanet Press, 1994)
Patrick Creagh, *Giacomo Leopardi: Moral Tales (Operette morali)*, (Manchester: Carcanet Press, 1983)

ALMA CLASSICS

ALMA CLASSICS aims to publish mainstream and lesser-known European classics in an innovative and striking way, while employing the highest editorial and production standards. By way of a unique approach the range offers much more, both visually and textually, than readers have come to expect from contemporary classics publishing.

～

To order any of our titles and for up-to-date information about our current and forthcoming publications, please visit our website on:

www.almaclassics.com